DO YOU PROMISE NOT TO TELL?

ALSO BY MARY JANE CLARK

Do You Want to Know a Secret?

Do you promise not to tell?

Mary Jane Clark

DOUBLEDAY DIRECT LARGE PRINT EDITION

ST. MARTIN'S PRESS ✿ NEW YORK

This Large Print Edition, prepared especially for Doubleday Direct, Inc., contains the complete unabridged text of the original Publisher's Edition.

ISBN 0-7394-0532-2

This Large Print Book carries the Seal of Approval of N.A.V.H.

❧ Acknowledgments

It takes a village to write and publish a book. I'd like to express my appreciation to the support population of *Do You Promise Not to Tell?*

Roberta Golubock took me to lunch at the Metropolitan Museum of Art while the Fabergé exhibit glittered. An idea was born and Roberta encouraged me to see it through to fruition.

Margaret Trombly, Director of the Forbes Museum, Associate Curator Robin Troemer-Brenner and George Tempro, Director of Administration, helped me with my early research on "Fauxbergé". Geza Von Hapsburg, Thomas Hoving, and the late Robert Woolley assisted too, with their respective tomes on Fabergé, art forgery, and auctions.

Norma Nutman and the late Deena Teitlebaum guided me through Brighton Beach as I tried to absorb the local color of "Little Odessa."

Margot Dennedy, Director of Security at Sotheby's, helped me find the one spot to get away with murder in a world class auction house without security cameras watching.

An FBI agent, who wishes to remain nameless, generously volunteered inside information on how today's Federal Bureau of Investigation works. I promise not to tell.

Louise and Joel Albert, Cathy and David Holmes and Barbara and Reginald Brack opened their "writer's retreats" to me.

Father Paul Holmes was my sounding board, hole-finder, and cheerleader, "egging" me on as I labored to make deadline. His editorial help made the book better.

Laura Dail, my agent and friend, seems to be thinking constantly of my career, which frees me up to think about my writing. I always feel I am in good hands with Laura and her enthusiastic assistant, Francheska Farinacci.

The St. Martin's Press team is led by Sally Richardson, who has made me feel quite special. My editor Jennifer Weis, her assistant, Joanna Jacobs, publicist Walter Halee and paperback quarterback Matthew Shear tackle their work hard, determined to score. My thanks to them and everyone at St. Martin's who worked on this project.

Frances Twoomey, what would I do without you?

Louise Albert, Joy Blake, Liz Flock, Cathy White Haffler, Katharine Hayden, Elizabeth Kaledin and Steve Simring: the ones I called when I was ready to shave my head. That happened alot.

Doris and Fred Behrends, my parents, constantly tried to help me.

Finally and always, Elizabeth and David, my children. They bear with their mother. I love you both, very, very much.

🌿 JUST FOR ELIZABETH . . . 🌿

My sparkling, intricate, miraculous treasure

Do you promise not to tell?

❧ Prologue

Why hassle with buying a gun when you can just cruise the aisles of Home Depot? It's all there.

A box of heavy-duty black plastic garbage bags was thrown into the wire shopping cart. Industrial Strength, the package boasted.

No one would miss Misha—at least no one that the police would bother trying to satisfy.

Slowly up and down the busy aisles. Pruning shears. Big ones. Into the basket they went.

Either you're on the team, or you're not, Misha.

So many axes, so little time. A salesman in an orange, bib-fronted apron appeared amid the axes.

"Can I help you?"

"Yes. I'm doing some yard work. I have to clear some trees and brush."

"How thick are the tree trunks?"

The salesman was assessed. "A little thicker than your waist."

The salesman selected a large, wooden-handled ax from the bin. "This one's a beauty. Double-edged. When one side gets dull, you just flip to the other."

"Okay."

"You said you have to clear some brush, too? It's a waste of your energy to use an ax as heavy as this one if you don't have to. You'd better have a smaller hatchet in your toolbox."

The hatchet found a home on top of the garbage bags.

"You'll want one of these files, too. That way, you can keep your tools keen. You'd be surprised at how much easier your job is when they're razor sharp."

In went a shiny new hammer for good luck.

It was essential to get out while the going was good. Many people would get away with their crimes if they just knew when to stop. Instead, their egos got in the way. You gotta know when to quit.

The pimply-faced high-school kid at the register scanned the tools that would make Misha . . . well, "go all to pieces."

The kid looked up and felt a chill creep up his spine. He ignored it.

"Spring cleanup, huh?"

Chapter 1

Farrell Slater knew her days were numbered. Her contract was up and Range Bullock, executive producer of *KEY Evening Headlines*, didn't like her. A lethal combination. Unless she could redeem herself, Farrell knew her contract would not be renewed and her days as one of the producers of the network's highly-rated evening-news broadcast would be over unless she could pull a journalistic rabbit out of a hat.

She'd even started going to church again. Funny how worry led one back to the kneeler. On the way to the office this morning, Farrell had stopped for ashes at St. Gabriel's. It was the first time in years she'd bothered. Might as well start the Lenten season off right. Having God on her side right now wouldn't hurt.

How the mighty had fallen. Eight years ago, as just a thirty-year-old, Farrell had been the talk of KEY News, having won three Emmy Awards in one season—industry recognition for her outstanding achievements in television news production. Everyone had loved her then, everyone had wanted to be her friend. She was a hot property, admired and sought after by her colleagues.

What had happened?

Part of it, she had to admit to herself, was that she hadn't been able to sustain the momentum and enthusiasm for her job. She had started to coast—just slightly at first, then a little bit more. So, to some degree it was her own fault she was where she was. But not entirely.

There was no doubt in Farrell's mind. Her boss detested her. Was there any way she could redeem herself? Did she want to? Bullock had written her off. The stories he was assigning to Farrell now were always "below the line," iffy stories listed way down on the morning's rundown, beneath the pieces sure to make air.

Occasionally one of Farrell's stories developed into something more than Bullock had anticipated. The executive producer was then forced, grudgingly, to give it a slot in the *Evening Headlines* lineup. If the piece came out well, Bullock credited its depth, creativity, and impact to the correspondent. If the piece came up short, Producer Farrell, ever the goat, got the blame.

Hanging her violet wool coat on the back of the door, Farrell, dressed in a simple turtleneck and black wool slacks, headed for her desk in the office she shared with Bullock's pet producer, Dean Cohen. Farrell lifted a cup of coffee from the Strokos Delicatessen's brown paper bag and studying her office mate, tried to remember what it was like to be the favored one.

Dean certainly wasn't any smarter or more aggressive than Farrell. His pieces were solid, never outstanding. But Dean was a skilled player in the KEY political game. He knew when to keep his mouth shut. Farrell did not. His sucking up to Range Bullock made Farrell want to gag.

"Happy Ash Wednesday," Dean nodded,

acknowledging the black smudge on Farrell's forehead.

"That's a contradiction in terms," Farrell corrected.

"Oh yeah, right. Ashes to ashes, dust to dust, and all that." Dean turned his attention back to his *New York Times*.

Now, why had she done that? She could have just smiled and said a simple thank-you. That's what most people would have done. But no. She had to put Dean in his place. It was a constant game of one-upmanship between them and she knew it. It didn't play well.

Perhaps if she were prettier, she could get away with it. But Farrell wasn't a conventionally pretty woman. Quirky, maybe—exotic, on a good day. She'd known since she was a little girl that she would make her way in life with her strongest asset, her brain. A coarse cloud of black curly hair crowned her high forehead. Large (almost too large) brown eyes gave her a look of wide-eyed wonder—not very reassuring in the television news business. The appearance of control could be more important than actual control.

Booting up her computer, Farrell groaned

inwardly as she viewed her lot for the day. How could she change Bullock's mind when he kept assigning her the dreck? The Fabergé auction over at Churchill's?

Below the line.

❧ Chapter 2

Pat struggled to stay seated. Please, God, just let the bidding go up.

The gavel snapped crisply. "Sold! To number four-ten. Fifteen thousand dollars for the Fabergé brooch."

Patricia Devereaux craned her auburn head, eager to see who had captured Olga's treasured crescent pin. Searching the crowd, she saw movement two rows ahead. Sitting on one of the folding chairs in the venerable Churchill's auction gallery, a wraithlike old woman dressed entirely in black smoothly replaced her green auction paddle in her lap. As the woman rose to leave, Pat got a better look.

Luminous dark eyes peered out from her

magnolia-skinned face. The woman's raven hair could not be untinted, but Pat suspected that years ago the shiny black had been its natural color. In her time, she must have been a real beauty, Pat decided.

But now the former beauty would be wearing Olga's brooch. Pat felt a tug of sadness. Dear Olga. How many times had the tiny Russian woman lovingly attached that pin to the collar of her carefully starched linen blouses? Olga had cherished the white enamel crescent studded with tiny sapphires—a gift from her father who had once worked in the studios of the famed jeweler Carl Fabergé. If an old woman was to wear this unique pin, Pat preferred that it be Olga.

Fabergé. The Imperial jeweler to the last Romanov czars.

Pat and her nineteen-year-old son Peter watched the distinguished-looking auctioneer standing at the raised walnut platform stationed in front of the large room. Well-dressed men and women spoke softly into the telephones at desks banking either side of the auctioneer's podium. Their job was to efficiently express bids made by potential buyers not on the floor of the salesroom.

The auctioneer expertly moved through

the numbered items in the Churchill's catalogue. A small copper ashtray embossed
with the Russian Imperial Eagles went for
fourteen hundred dollars. A pair of silver Fabergé asparagus tongs earned over its es-
timate of two thousand. A silver table lighter
in the form of a crouching monkey went for
twenty-five thousand. The monkey's expressive face and lined forehead had clearly
charmed its new owner.

"What do we have for the gold cigarette
case?"

Pat studied the picture of the cigarette
case featured in her program. The fourteen-
karat golden cover was monogrammed and
featured a diamond-set Imperial Eagle.
When pressed, the sapphire thumbpiece
opened the elegant container. Beautiful.

"Four thousand once.

"Four thousand twice.

"Sold! Four thousand dollars to number
one-ninety-six."

Pat recognized the buyer. It was the same
man who had purchased Olga's silver cigarette case at last year's auction. The tall,
pleasant-looking man was wearing a tweed
sports jacket. She guessed him to be about

forty-five, maybe older. As she studied him, he looked in her direction and smiled.

Did he remember her from last year?

"That's Professor Kavanagh! My Russian Studies prof." Peter was out of his seat and headed for the cigarette-case buyer. The men shook hands and Pat watched as Peter gestured toward her and she could see his lips form the words, *That's my mother*. Pat thought the professor looked surprised, maybe even pleased, to hear the information.

Pat was used to it. People often commented that it had to be impossible for her to be the mother of a nineteen-year-old. But she'd been Peter's age when her only child was born.

As Pat looked on, she was surprised herself. Seton Hall University must be paying good salaries. Fabergé cigarette cases didn't come cheap. The men shook hands again and Peter came back to join his mother. His face was flushed with pleasure.

"This is great, Mom," he whispered. "Meeting my favorite professor at a Churchill's auction—I think he was surprised to see one of his students at something like this."

Pat enjoyed her son's enthusiasm. Peter

was such an earnest kid. She often found herself hoping he wouldn't get hurt.

"I told him about your shop, Mom. He said he'd like to stop in sometime."

"Great, sweetheart," she whispered back; but she was more interested in what was happening at the front of the room.

The numbered treasures continued to fetch small fortunes and Pat felt the electricity building in the crowd as the star attraction slowly made its way closer to the auction block. Then, it rolled into view. The audience sat up straighter in their chairs and a low, reverential roar swept over the tension-charged room. The television news crews stationed throughout the gallery rolled their video cameras.

Pat shivered at the auctioneer's announcement.

"Ladies and gentlemen, the Moon Egg."

Chapter 3

Safe from the curious stares of the eyes below in the auction gallery, there was privacy in the Churchill's skybox. In the skybox, one could see out, but no one could see in.

The bidding on the Moon Egg was heated. From the floor, on the phones, the price went higher and higher.

The auctioneer entered the bids as he received them, and the price rose higher still.

Whatever it took, the skybox bidder was determined to have the egg. It was meant to be.

Chapter 4

"What else should we shoot, boss?"

Tall and lanky, B. J. D'Elia stood poised with his video camera, ready for Farrell's cue.

"Hold on a minute, Beej, I'm thinking."

Farrell stood at the side of the crowded gallery and debated with herself. This was a better story than she had originally anticipated. Should she snag Churchill's president, Clifford Montgomery, for a unilateral interview? What was the point? Range was never going to buy a full piece on the sale of the Moon Egg. He wasn't going to give one minute and thirty seconds of his valuable *Evening Headlines* airtime to this story. Farrell had known this the minute he'd assigned the piece to her.

A voice-over, at best. Anchor Eliza Blake would narrate fifteen or twenty seconds of video of the Fabergé egg and the auction scene, telling the audience that the egg had sold for a record six million dollars.

But it was a far more compelling story than Farrell had first thought. Frustrated, Farrell was certain she could construct a more interesting piece. She'd get some file video from the film and tape library. She remembered some old black-and-white newsreel stuff KEY News had obtained of the Romanovs at play on their royal yacht, the *Standart*. Shortly thereafter, Czar Nicholas II and his family had been forced from the Alexander palace and sent into exile, only to be executed a few months later by the ruthless Bolsheviks. Their royal bodies had been doused with acid and buried in a pit in the darkness of the Russian woods.

She could ask Robbie to pull it for her.

The story of the long-lost Moon Egg and how it had been discovered decades after its creation as an Easter gift for Czarina Alexandra from her devoted husband, was a producer's dream. It had all the elements: romance, wealth, betrayal, tragedy. *I can't miss with this story*, thought Farrell. *It's great TV.*

Farrell pulled out her cell phone and stabbed the numbers that would connect her with the Fishbowl, the *Evening Headlines* command center. Dean Cohen picked up.

"Cohen," he answered crisply.

Swell. The fair-haired boy busy kissing up to Master Bullock. Dean was forever trawling around the Fishbowl. He thrived on hanging out in the executive producer's glass-enclosed office.

"Dean, it's Farrell."

"How'd the auction go?"

"Great. Can I talk to Range?"

"He's on another line."

"I'll hold."

Farrell held on, her eyes scanning the auction gallery. She saw a tall, pretty woman gathering up her things and rising from her seat. An even taller teenaged boy got up along with her. There was something familiar about her.

Pat! She looked almost the same as she had the last time Farrell had seen her. How long ago was that? Farrell's mind searched. Could it be almost twenty years? And that must be Peter—he had been just a baby when last she'd seen him! *My God.*

"Bullock here," snapped the voice in the earpiece. Bullock's abrupt, clipped manner always caught Farrell off guard.

"Range, it's Farrell."

"I know who it is."

Of course he knew who it was. How stupid of her to identify herself again. When would she learn that, with Bullock, she should dispense with the niceties? He just wanted her to get to the point.

Farrell hated herself as she heard herself stammer, "Well, the Moon Egg just went for six million."

"And?"

"Well, I think we could do a good story on it."

"Why?"

"The whole history of the thing is fascinating."

"Who bought it?"

"A telephone bidder who wants to remain anonymous."

There was a short pause on the line. Farrell pictured Bullock checking his computer screen.

"We're heavy tonight. Best we can do is give it a twenty-second v/o."

The connection was broken.

✦ Chapter 5

"The Bowl doesn't want it," Farrell announced, shrugging. "Do you mind, Beej? I'm going to take a cab back to the Broadcast Center now."

"Damn, I love the shot I got of that doorman in the Russian cossack getup out front. Cool costume. Oh well, you go ahead, Farrell. I'll see you back there."

B. J. D'Elia continued to pack up his video gear as he watched Farrell walk away, her shoulders slumped. It would only take about ten minutes to break down and stow away the tripod, lights, and wires and load them into the crew car parked outside Churchill's on Madison Avenue. Farrell knew that. And with no story to produce for tonight's broadcast, there was certainly no big rush to get back to KEY. She must want to be on her own, not in the mood for company or conversation. Who could blame her? Farrell couldn't get herself arrested on *Evening Headlines.*

Twenty-eight years old, Bartolomeo Joseph D'Elia loved working in television news. Forty hours a week, plus all the overtime he could get, he was paid for his passion. Going out to cover whatever assignment blew his way, B. J. lived by his wits, his skills, and the seat of his pants.

Was he lucky, or what! He thought of that all the time. Most poor stiffs hated to get up in the morning, dragged themselves to their boring jobs, counting the hours until it was time to go home. Then they ate some dinner, watched a lot of television, and went to bed, only to get up and do it all over again. When he thought about what life must be like for those guys, he shuddered. B. J. knew he was one of the fortunate few who actually looked forward to work each day.

Farrell, on the other hand, was struggling, and everyone at KEY knew it. Gossip was elevated to an art form. Who was in favor, who was screwing up, who was on the rise, who had already seen his or her best days. Career bumps and rough patches sustained the voracious appetites of the newshounds. They watched with the same fascination of rubberneckers on the highway who slow down to see if the passengers in a car wreck are going to come out alive—mesmerized and grateful, (perhaps "happy" would be the right word) that they were safe, at least for today.

KEY News was no longer the cradle-to-grave operation it had once proudly been in years gone by. In the past, when a longtime employee had served the company well, the news division would keep him on staff when his most productive days were behind him. *You took care of us, now we'll take care of you.* Not anymore.

Corporate loyalty cut both ways. Employees sensed the company wasn't committed to the workers the way it had been once. Many employees didn't give as much as a result. Why bust your hump for the company when it wasn't going to be there for you?

That's why B. J. was a standout. He always went the extra mile, treating every story he worked on like it had Emmy Award–nomination potential. He paid attention to the details, put thought and energy into each camera shot. Producers loved to work with him. When B. J. had done the camera work in the field, they knew that there would be great material to work with in the editing room. Producers always asked to have him assigned to their stories.

He was also a lot of fun. Quick-witted, well-read, and street-smart, he was able to size up a situation and, when it got tense, diffuse it with humor. In a world where everyone took themselves very seriously, B. J. could be counted on to put things in perspective with some comic relief. But today his attempts at humor had failed with Farrell. She hadn't even smiled at any of his wisecracks.

He finished winding up the last bit of black rubber-coated electrical wire and stowed it in the camera gear case. He forgot Farrell as once more he looked to the front of the auction gallery.

That young Asian woman staffing the telephone bank was a babe. He wondered for about five seconds if he should go for it.

Chapter 6

The auction over, Pat and Peter went down-stairs to the Churchill's checkroom to collect their coats. Professor Kavanagh joined them on line. He extended his hand to Pat.

"Let me introduce myself, Mrs. Devereaux. I'm Tim Kavanagh, Peter's Russian Studies prof."

Pat shook his hand, smiling warmly. He had a good, firm handshake. Pat liked that.

"So very nice to meet you. Peter's always talking about your class. It's his favorite."

"Your son has a real enthusiasm for Russian history. It's uncommon for someone his age, especially since I would have to guess he doesn't have much Russian blood in him."

"You'd be guessing right. Peter comes from a long line of Irish men and women. But he's never taken much of an interest in that part of his heritage."

Peter corrected his mother.

"Mom, I'm an American. I know about American history."

Pat nodded. "Of course, Peter. But it doesn't hurt to pay a little more attention to what our forebears went through."

Their turn came to pick up their coats and, buttoning her camel-hair reefer, Pat turned to say good-bye to Professor Kavanagh.

"It was so nice to meet you."

"Same here. You know, it's lunchtime, and seeing all that beautiful Fabergé has really stimulated my appetite. How about I take you two out for an all-American hamburger?"

Before Pat could decline, Peter chimed, "Great!"

Pat laughed. *Why shouldn't I go?* she asked herself. Often when a man asked her out, she made some excuse about her business or her parental responsibilities. She'd finally admitted to herself that she just didn't want to fall in love again, to be involved with someone who could complicate her life. But this would be safe enough. Peter and his teacher. A hamburger. There'd be no pressure. Professor Kavanagh was looking at her expectantly.

"Sounds good. A cheeseburger would hit the spot right about now."

As they exited to the street through the heavy glass door, Pat felt a tap on her shoulder. She turned expectantly.

"My God—Farrell! Farrell Slater!" Pat reached to hug the other woman. "I haven't seen you in . . . forever!"

❧ Chapter 7

Tony didn't really mind wearing the cossack costume. It sure worked like a charm on the little old ladies who were the big tippers. He was just grateful that Clifford Montgomery had decided that Russian Season at Churchill's was February and March, not July and August.

He stood before the imposing entrance of the auction house wearing a long, marine-blue wool coat with red collar and cuffs, and slouchy black boots. A sword hung at his waist and slings of bullets crisscrossed his chest. A holster held a fake gun on his hip.

He'd even let his beard grow in anticipation of this month. Tony wanted to look as authentic as he could.

What a crowd this Fabergé stuff was bringing in! Montgomery and the board of directors must be pretty happy. Good for business. And what was good for Churchill's was great for Tony.

The more customers who came to the auction house, the more tips Tony made. At about thirty thousand dollars, his salary was meager by New York City standards. But in a good year he could triple his income by charming and pampering the wealthy clientele.

He hailed cabs and checked coats and packages, ingratiating himself to the patrons who expected to be accommodated and were prepared to pay for it. He accompanied old men and women and blind people across busy Madison Avenue; not because he'd get paid for it, but because it was the right thing to do. Many times, though, it did pay off—not because these vulnerable creatures were wealthy Churchill's customers, but because the regular auction-house clients took notice of his good deeds and rewarded him for it. Ten- and twenty-dollar bills added up quickly and it was easy not to declare cash for tax purposes.

Christmastime was the best. People were the most generous then. But when there were special theme months at Churchill's, and the same customers returned to each session in a series of auctions, they soon felt comfortable with the pleasant doorman. Tony took good care of them and, honoring their part of the unspoken contract, they slid the bills into his gloved hand.

"Good morning, Mrs. Busby." He opened the door for yet another attractive, well-groomed woman.

Tony enjoyed his vantage point in front of Churchill's. He saw everyone as they arrived and when they departed. He always made an effort to learn their names. The customers liked that.

Chapter 8

Life was raw in "Little Odessa," or Brighton Beach, as it was named on the map of the borough of Brooklyn. Brighton Beach Avenue, the main thoroughfare, bustled with intense, hardened faces hurrying to their destinations. Only the old and the very young moved at a more relaxed pace.

The avenue was dotted with open-air fruit stands. The Russian immigrants chose their apples, bananas, and pears with a level of concentration and wonder. It had not been like this in the Old Country. Never this abundance of fresh produce, ripe and unspoiled.

At the corner newsstands, the *New York Post*, the *Daily News*, and *People* magazine were displayed alongside Russian newspapers. Along the sidewalks, people set up their own small stands to sell books printed in Cyrillic, the Russian alphabet.

The street signs were in Cyrillic, too. So were the signs that labeled the drugstores, five-and-dimes, and jewelry shops. The markets stocked the traditional Russian foodstuffs: black bread, fish, and pastries. Lots and lots of pastries. After decades of deprivation, the Russian immigrant loved to indulge his sweet tooth.

On the boardwalk that ran parallel to Brighton Beach Avenue and alongside the cold, gray Atlantic Ocean, older men and women took their daily exercise in the late-winter sun. Conversations were all in Russian. Often the discussions centered on the crime in Little Odessa.

Some things would never change. In the Old Country, the government officials were always on the take. In America, the Russian mafia demanded its own pound of flesh. Too many times, the talk on the boardwalk was about some poor, defiant shopkeeper who'd been shot when he didn't come up with the protection money. The criminals wanted a piece of everything.

In a rented room over the Primorski Restaurant, Misha Grinkov bent over his workbench. He had come to the United States so many years ago, heading straight for Brighton Beach. Not speaking a word of English, he wanted to go to the only place in America he knew of where language would not be a problem for him.

But when seeking employment in his new country, he had gone back to the business he knew best. He took a subway to Manhattan and to the sleek world of the Upper East Side, heading straight for La Russie Imperiale, the venerated Fifth Avenue antique store. La Russie Imperiale specialized in the sale of Russian antiquities, artifacts and jewelry from the days before the Communists had seized control of the largest country in the world.

The owner, Konstantin Kaledin, had spoken to him in Russian. Misha had described his work in St. Petersburg, and gingerly unwrapped a black felt-covered bundle that he had carried and guarded carefully on the long journey to his new home. When Kaledin had examined Misha's expert work, he had hired the immigrant on the spot.

The very next day, Kaledin set Misha to work executing his specialty—enameling. There was a constant stream of cigarette cases, letter openers, tea-glass holders, kovshes, frames, and candlesticks that needed to be repaired. Misha mixed the compound of glass and metal oxides and heated it until it began to melt. That was painstakingly applied and fused to a prepared metal surface which had already been engraved. The extremely high temperatures necessary to melt the enamel taxed the skills of most enamel experts, but Misha had always enjoyed the challenge. During his long apprenticeship in Russia, he had spent every minute he could, experimenting with layering enamels, inserting gold-leaf patterns between the layers, and engraving decorations on the metal surface before applying the enamel. Misha lovingly polished the enamel with chamois leather for many, many hours. He did it willingly, knowing that the extra work made for a more beautiful finish.

One day Mr. Kaledin, his face even more serious than usual, approached Misha at his workbench.

"I have a very unhappy customer. The enamel cracked on a very costly piece. I trust you enough to repair it."

So Misha Grinkov had come to see his first Fabergé egg in America.

For the next decade, Misha labored at La

Russie Imperiale, repairing the enamel on the beautiful pieces that came into the shop and picking up English from the other workers and the aging Konstantin Kaledin. A job at La Russie had cachet in the world of antiques. A sales position provided one with an opportunity to acquire a better education in Russian works of art than could ever be gained in any classroom or library.

There was one apprentice salesman back in those early years, a salesman who had eventually become Kaledin's right-hand man—a tall, well-spoken black man named Clifford Montgomery. Misha remembered how upset Kaledin had been when Montgomery had decided to leave the shop and go to work at Churchill's Auction House.

Chapter 9

Jack McCord hated Russian school. He found the language difficult and he had little aptitude for it. But he loved his job, thrived on the investigative work and puzzle-solving, and took great satisfaction in nailing the bad guys. Learning that damned Russian language was the price of admission to his profession.

The Cold War was over, but the Federal Bureau of Investigation still had reason to send select agents to Russian school. Though for decades the FBI graduates had worked in espionage and focused on the Soviet spies in the United States, McCord was assigned to the art-fraud division in the New York office. The spread of forged Russian art objects was virulent.

As he drove out to Brighton Beach in the early-morning hours, he cursed the budget cutbacks at the Bureau. There were never enough agents to do everything that needed to be done. A ridiculously strong argument had had to be made to his supervisor in order to have a surveillance team assigned to his case. Despite Jack's pleading, the boss didn't think Misha Grinkov was important enough to be watched around the clock.

"You'll have to do the best you can," Supervisor Roger Quick said.

Easy for Quick to say as he sat on his can, never having to leave the office. It had been a long time since Quick had been in the field, and it showed. Jack couldn't stand Quick, and it angered him that he had to take orders from the jerk.

But he controlled himself. He knew Quick was egging him on and would love to see Jack lose his temper. Again.

In the foggy grayness of the morning, Jack found a parking space around the corner from the Primorski Restaurant. He parked the car, locked it, and walked toward the coffee shop across the street.

Nothing would make that son of a bitch happier, Jack reflected as he crossed Brighton Beach Avenue. Quick wanted Jack to blow his stack, knowing that one more burst of uncontrolled temper would end Jack's career. The FBI didn't like loose cannons.

He'd be damned if he'd give Quick the satisfaction.

Jack took a seat in a booth that faced out to the street, ordered a cup of coffee, and waited for Misha.

Chapter 10

At her KEY News desk the morning after the auction, Farrell sipped her coffee and read the black-and-white account on the front page of the *Times*.

The Moon Egg, the last of the Imperial Easter Eggs commissioned by the czar Nicholas II for his wife, Alexandra, lost for decades in the chaos following the Russian revolution in 1917, was purchased yesterday by an unknown buyer for six million dollars at Churchill's auction gallery in New York. The creation of the egg was guided by Carl Fabergé, the best-known artist-jeweler of all time.

   The Moon Egg, fabricated of milky, translucent enamel over engraved gold, rests on dark blue clouds of carved lapis lazuli which rotate on a gold base. The design for the egg, recently unearthed in an old catalogue of Fabergé designs, called for the egg to open to reveal the Fabergé trademark "surprise"—in this case, a spray of diamonds which, at the triggering of a mechanism, shimmers to simulate a comet of shooting stars. Over time, the diamond surprise has disappeared from the Moon Egg.

The egg was never delivered to the czar since Nicholas, his wife Alexandra Feodorovna, and their five children were taken as prisoners by the Bolshevik revolutionaries. The entire family was executed the following year.

In the tumult that followed the overthrow of the Imperial family, many treasures were lost, stolen, or sold by the cash-poor new government. Carl Fabergé's jewelry-design book, from the St. Petersburg Archives, includes sketches of the planned egg but, until Churchill's announced the sale, the actual whereabouts, or even the existence, of the Moon Egg had been a mystery.

Over the years, varied objects of fantasy and function created at the House of Fabergé have turned up in unlikely places. Churchill's reports that the Moon Egg was discovered and purchased by the consignor at New York's Twenty-Sixth Street Flea Market late last year.

The discovery sent tremors of excitement throughout the art world. It had been expected that the Moon Egg would be purchased by the Forbes Magazine Collection, which retains twelve Fabergé Imperial Easter Eggs. The buyer, who bid by phone, wished to remain anonymous, according to Clifford Montgomery, president and specialist in charge of Russian Works of Art and Objects of Vertu at Churchill's.

Farrell took another sip of coffee, dribbling some on her starched white blouse. Slob! She was on a roll, all right. She stared at the color picture of the Moon Egg that accompanied the *Times* article and wished that Range's dislike of her hadn't clouded his decision. A full piece on the Moon Egg had been warranted on *Evening Headlines*. It was pretty pathetic when a personality clash dictated what the American viewing public saw on the evening news. But Farrell knew that was exactly what had happened.

Even KEY News president Yelena Gregory had taken note. Yelena, who had some Russian blood herself, had phoned to let Range know she wasn't pleased by the omission. Range must be kicking himself,

Farrell mused gleefully. The *New York Times* was gospel at KEY—and all the other networks had done full pieces on their evening broadcasts.

But Range could never blame himself. He was going to blame *her*.

Chapter 11

Misha answered the knock at the door of his small, hidden workshop in Brighton Beach, leaving his half-eaten sausage sandwich on his worktable.

"Don't you know you should ask who's there before opening the door? I could be anyone—the police, the Russian mafia . . . anyone."

Misha smiled wryly. "Yes, but I knew it be you. No one else ever comes here."

That's fortunate for me, unfortunate for you, thought the visitor.

Misha turned and gestured to his workbench, cleared of all but the sandwich, his jeweler's tools carefully hung on the wall rack above.

"As you can see, I am having some trouble starting on something new."

"Why do you think that is?"

"I tell you before, I want bigger piece of profits. You making fortune while Misha does all work," Misha said resentfully, staring at the jeweler's tools. "I only ask what fair."

"I know you do. Your work on the Moon Egg was perfection. So perfect that neither one of us should ever have to work on anything else. Six million dollars is a lot of money."

Misha turned to look at his visitor, a relieved smile on his face.

"So. You share with me?"

The hammer came down right in the middle of Misha's forehead. He never knew what hit him. Methodically each limb was hacked off, each fingertip removed, and his head cut off with the double-edged ax.

Chapter 12

If she were mine, I'd never let her go, Charlie Ferrino thought, as he smeared a fresh raisin bagel with cream cheese. Instead he said, "I've never understood how you can make a living selling other people's old junk."

Pat smiled and pulled a crisp *New York Times* from beneath the counter at Choo-Choo Charlie's Coffee Shop. Eagerly she noted the story about the auction was featured on the front page.

"Charlie, Charlie," chided Pat, her green eyes playful as she and her friend began their familiar morning dance. "It's not old junk! You know our slogan: 'The Consignment Depot—Everything of Quality and Character.' "

"Then why don't you just call it an antique shop?"

"Because our merchandise isn't necessarily antique. I've explained it before: I don't own the furniture, crystal, silver, or whatever else we have on sale. I'm selling it for the owners. They bring me their things, I display them in the shop, and when something sells, the owner and I split the purchase price . . . fifty-fifty."

Charlie filled a paper cup with steaming, fresh-brewed coffee, sprinkled the contents from a pink package of Sweet'N Low, and added some milk. He was wearing a blue baseball cap to cover his balding head, which was shaking from side to side.

"I don't know, Pat. I hear some of your prices are pretty steep. Why would anyone want to pay good money for secondhand stuff when they could afford to buy it new?"

Pat grinned. They both knew that Charlie understood the concept of fine things and antiques quite well. He just liked to tease her. Feigning exasperation, she tugged her auburn hair out from the sides of her head.

"Charlie, it's a good thing I'm crazy about you, because sometimes I just want to grab your shoulders and shake you."

Charlie carefully packed the wrapped bagel, coffee, and a napkin into a small brown paper bag.

I wish you would, he thought, admiring her as she walked away.

✿ Chapter 13

Peter didn't know what to do.

He lay on his single bed in Boland Hall, the large Seton Hall University freshman dormitory, staring at the ceiling, his arms crossed behind his head. The gray, rainy day outside the metal-rimmed window matched the college freshman's mood. He was deeply troubled.

Since the auction yesterday, something had been eating at him. The Moon Egg.

It sure was beautiful. The enamel work and all the jewels were awesome. And when it sold for six million dollars, Peter heard the man sitting in the row behind him comment, "Well worth it."

It would have been. Except that it was a fake.

Peter was sure of it.

He rolled over and, closing his eyes, buried his face in his pillow. God, what should he do?

He didn't want to tell Olga. She was so old, and she had already been through so much in her life. Peter didn't want the old lady to have any more problems in her remaining days.

And she had made him swear that he wouldn't tell.

He remembered the afternoon clearly. Olga had set out tea and her homemade eggplant caviar as she did whenever he came to visit. But from the moment Peter entered her little apartment that day, he sensed that something was different.

Olga's eyes had shone brightly as the two of them sat in her small living room, Olga reminiscing about the old days. She told him about her family, now long dead, and about how it had been growing up as a young girl in St. Petersburg after the Communists had taken over. She talked about her father's re-signed acceptance of how their comfortable world had changed forever.

Gone was their spacious apartment in St. Petersburg and their charming *dacha* in the countryside. Gone was the well-stocked kitchen with its ample supply of good wine and vodka in the pantry. Gone were the fine dresses and well-tailored suits and the many fur coats in the hall closet.

Then, in the bitterness of another unforgiving Russian winter, her mother died.

A tear had come to Olga's eye as she spoke of her father. She had watched her father eaten away more by the inability to use his gift than by the loss of material wealth. In the Russia of the Communists, there had been no place for the "frivolous" creation of beautiful things.

Then she pulled herself from her chair and slowly walked toward her bedroom.

"Come with me."

Peter followed the old lady as she headed to the closet. She opened the door and gestured.

Peter got down on his knees and reached toward the back of the closet. Beneath a wool blanket, he felt something soft and plush. He pulled the box free, rose, and handed the yellow velvet container to Olga.

"You promise not to tell what I show you? My father make this, but he also take from studio when Communists come."

Peter nodded solemnly. "I promise."

Olga's hands shook as she opened the

golden box, and Peter gasped at its contents.

"Imperial Easter Egg. Czar have it made for present for Czarina Alexandra."

Olga held out the box toward Peter. Peter carefully lifted the blue-and-white egg from its yellow nest.

Slowly he turned the egg over in his hands, his breath taken away by its cool beauty.

"Open it."

Peter studied the egg, trying to figure out how it opened. He looked up at Olga, a quizzical expression on his face.

"Here, I do for you."

Olga took the egg from him. She pressed on a gold bead that was part of the design, and the egg split open.

A shower of delicately connected diamonds quivered inside.

"Is made after Halley's comet. Comet appear in Europe before czar overthrown. Was sign—telegram from God."

The Consignment Depot opened at ten, but Pat liked to get there at least an hour earlier to get organized. Once she opened the doors for customers, she often didn't have a minute to herself until she locked up at six o'clock. Still, she just barely paid her bills each month. She'd never been able to get ahead.

Pat stood, breakfast and *New York Times* in hand, on the wooden porch that rimmed the charming Victorian frame house that was home to the consignment shop. Fifteen years ago she had gone way out on a financial limb to buy the old, run-down house in suburban Westwood, New Jersey. But as always, when she looked at it, now so lovingly restored, she was glad she had taken the chance.

After Allan had died, Pat had missed him so much there were times she didn't think she could keep going. But she had put all of her energy and the proceeds from a small insurance policy into fixing up the old house and starting her own business, and somehow, to her amazement, she'd gotten through the worst. She'd always love this old place. It had saved her. Barely.

The house, the business—but more importantly, Peter—had kept Pat going. Now he was a freshman in college; but then he'd been just four years old . . . a little boy facing childhood and the complicated growth to manhood without a father to stand by him. It was so unfair.

Uneasily, Pat inspected the paint job. The body of the house was a pale apple green, with elaborate gingerbread trim done in an unexpected shade of raspberry. Before selecting the paint, Pat had researched carefully, wanting to be true to the colors used at the time the house was built. She had been surprised to learn that people had been painting their houses whimsical colors at the end of the nineteenth century.

She sighed. The house needed another painting. And that would be costly. All the scrollwork and tiny patterned shingles had to be colored carefully by hand. What a miserable drag it was, worrying about money all these years.

Letting herself in through the beveled glass-paneled front door, Pat knew who would be waiting for her on the other side.

"Emily!" she cried, as she knelt and buried her forehead into the collie's long, honey-colored fur. "Good girl! Good girl! I can see you are taking good care of everything for me. I know I can count on you. Come on, Em. I'll let you out."

The collie followed her mistress to the tiny kitchen at the rear of the house and eagerly made her way through the door that led to the backyard. Insurance regulations called for the Consignment Depot to be electrically alarmed, but Pat always had trouble with the damned thing. Emily was the safety backup and Pat had the feeling the dog liked doing her part.

Pat walked back to the living room and surveyed her shop with pride. The plum-colored walls were a good foil for just about anything she hung on them . . . paintings, etchings, mirrors, sconces and, sometimes, just empty frames, if they were interesting enough on their own.

Mirrors. We're down on mirrors, and

they're always good sellers. She hoped someone would bring one in today.

She switched on all the lamps, both upstairs and down, plumped a needlepoint pillow on a tufted settee that sat beside the fireplace, and straightened a vanilla candle that tilted in the silver candelabra on the mantel. Smoothing the corner of a beautifully woven kilim that Emily had accidentally flipped back from the aged oak floor, Pat was satisfied the shop looked in order.

Back in the kitchen, Pat unwrapped her breakfast and opened up the newspaper. She relished the headline, remembering the excitement at Churchill's salesroom.

MOON EGG FETCHES SIX MILLION DOLLARS.

As she read the article, Pat's thoughts turned to Farrell Slater. How weird to meet again at an auction gallery after all these years.

They'd been grammar-school classmates and had been, at one time, inseparable. But Farrell had gone to parochial high school, while Pat had gone to Westwood High. When Farrell went away to college, Pat married Allan just after graduation.

Too young, too young to get married, everyone had clucked.

She considered that Peter was, today, older than she had been when she'd married his father. Pat admitted that they'd been young. But she didn't regret her decision. Not one single day of their too-short time together.

Her friend Farrell had gone on to the big leagues. A producer at KEY News! What an exciting life Farrell must be leading.

And yet, Farrell hadn't looked very happy at Churchill's yesterday. She'd been friendly enough when introduced to Tim Kavanagh, and seemed genuinely pleased to see Pat and Peter, exclaiming her amazement that the little baby she had known had grown into such a handsome young man. But Pat sensed a troubled air about her.

When Pat had suggested that Farrell drive out sometime to see the Consignment Depot, Pat had been surprised by Farrell's enthusiasm at her invitation. With a job that took her all around the world, that opened doors to interviews with some of the most fascinating people of our time, Pat couldn't imagine why in the world her old friend would be so interested in coming out to visit a consignment shop.

Chapter 15

Peter lingered after his Russian Studies lecture in Fahy Hall. He wanted to talk to Professor Kavanagh.

He hadn't come to his decision lightly. He wanted to tell his mother about his fears about the Moon Egg. He'd often gone to her when things bothered him and she was never too busy to listen. Together they'd always been able to figure things out.

But this was different. This wasn't about a Spanish progress report or being caught smoking with his buddies in the fifth grade. Those things, which had loomed large at the time, were so trivial now.

A six-million-dollar art forgery—that was in a whole other league. And Peter knew this was way beyond his or his mother's depth.

That, and the fact she had enough to worry about. He knew it hadn't been easy for her, raising him alone and always anxious about money. Though she'd tried to keep it from him, many nights when his mother had thought he was asleep, Peter had quietly gotten out of bed and checked on her as she sat at the kitchen table, engrossed in paying bills and going over the Consignment Depot ledger. She'd been unaware as he'd watched her sigh deeply, running her fingers through her hair, her brow knitted with worry.

Yet anytime he brought up the subject of their family finances, she'd always smile and say, "Don't worry, honey. Everything is fine."

He knew her workouts were a way to release anxiety.

No. He didn't want to saddle her with this. He was a man now. It was time for him to take more responsibility, make life easier for her. He would figure out what to do on his own.

Professor Kavanagh was gathering up his lecture notes as Peter approached the teacher's desk. Kavanagh smiled when he saw the young man.

"What did you think of the lecture today, Peter? Those Romanov czars pulled some pretty atrocious stunts, didn't they?"

"Yeah, it was pretty interesting, Dr. Kavanagh. But I was wondering if I could talk to you about something else."

Kavanagh looked at his student with concern. "Your mother's all right, isn't she?"

"Oh yeah. She's fine. But I don't know what to do about something, and I, uh, was hoping you could give me some advice."

🎗 Chapter 16

COME SEE ME AFTER THE BROADCAST TO-NIGHT.

Farrell's chest tightened and her mind raced as she read the e-mail from Range Bullock.

She could probably get a job over at *Dateline*. Farrell had heard that NBC had two hundred producers on staff to get their news-magazine show on the air five nights a week. But she didn't want to go to NBC or any of the other networks. She liked KEY News. It was home. Despite her problems with Range, she wasn't interested in learning her way around another network's news operation at this stage of the game.

Sure, the mechanics were the same and her knowledge was easily transferable. A satellite feed was a satellite feed whether at KEY, CBS, or ABC. Videotape was edited the same way wherever you went. Farrell had a Rolodex of contacts and sources that would work for her just as well at any news division.

It was learning a whole new cast of characters that didn't appeal to Farrell. At KEY News, she could pick up the phone and know just who to call to get done what she needed done. She knew personnel history, who was good, who was mediocre. She didn't want to move to another network and be forced to memorize the names and jobs of scores of new people. She could find her way around the maze of the KEY News Broadcast Center with her eyes shut. She didn't want to start all over again somewhere else.

But if something didn't change, that's exactly what Farrell would be doing. She knew Range wanted her out.

Chapter 17

Bunny's back room was crowded at lunch-time, with students from Seton Hall and other village residents and shopkeepers. A short drive from campus on South Orange Avenue, the bar and restaurant was popular with anyone who wanted some good, cheesy, New Jersey pizza. Up front, men sipped midday beers at the old wooden bar, while college students hung out and chowed down at booths in the back.

Peter and Professor Kavanagh sat in a booth in the corner.

"I think you'll have to tell your mother about this, Peter."

Peter helped himself to another pizza slice from the raised metal pie plate in the center of the table. Watching the young man shake red hot-pepper flakes and garlic powder over his pizza, the professor noticed that Peter's worries weren't affecting his appetite any.

"My mother already has enough to worry about. Besides, I promised Olga I wouldn't tell anyone about her egg." Peter looked uncomfortable. "I've already broken my promise by telling you."

Professor Kavanagh considered Peter's predicament as he sipped his cold Budweiser. Before it was over, many people were going to have to know Olga's secret.

"Peter, we're talking about art fraud and millions of dollars here."

"I know. I know." Peter closed his eyes and rested his head on the back of the booth. He heard a loud conversation at the booth behind him, about the Seton Hall Pirates and their March Madness prospects. How he wished he could be concentrating on something as simple as basketball right now. But he knew the professor was right. He should tell his mother about all of this. Then she could decide what to do and how to tell Olga.

Tim Kavanagh peeled several singles from his billfold and tucked them under the pizza stand for the waitress.

"Look. If you want, I'll come with you and we can both tell your mother. Would that make it easier?"

Peter considered the professor's offer. It would be good to have someone there to help figure things out, someone to lean on a little. That might be great for his mother . . . and for him.

"If I decide to tell her, I'll let you know."

 Chapter 18

It had been a good day, but Pat was anxious to finish up and get over to the American Woman health club to work out. With Emily curled snuggling at her feet, Pat was entering the day's receipts into the Consignment Depot sales ledger when she heard the creaking of the front door opening. She rose from her desk tucked at the rear of the shop and, seeing who it was, Pat smiled with pleasure.

"Olga! I was hoping you'd make it in today."

The wizened old woman looked brittle and worn as she crept toward Pat, but when she smiled back, it was clear that she was pleased by Pat's welcome.

"Here, Olga. Come try out this big wing chair we just got in."

As Pat helped Olga into the upholstered seat, she noted that the aged lady looked thinner and smaller than when she'd seen her just a few weeks ago, when she'd picked up the old woman's brooch to take it to Churchill's.

Churchill's reputation as a first-class auction house was well deserved. Over the last few years, as she had handled the arrangements for Olga to sell her pieces of Fabergé, Pat had been impressed with Churchill's staff and their attention to detail. Each object to be auctioned was inspected, studied, and authenticated by Churchill's experts. The auction house staked its considerable reputation on the fact that Churchill's could be trusted to reveal everything known about works of art, furniture, and decorative objects on the auction block.

That's why Pat had taken the pin into Churchill's weeks ago. Clifford Montgomery insisted on inspecting all Fabergé items himself before they could be listed in the Churchill's auction catalogue.

"Why don't I make us some tea?"

Olga nodded gratefully, and Pat went to the small kitchen and put the kettle to boil on the electric stove. She took some short-bread cookies from a tin canister and arranged them on an old pink-and-white Dresden plate. When the whistle blew, she fixed tea for them both, serving the dark amber liquid the way Olga liked it, in a glass instead of a cup.

"Hmmm, that is good." Olga sipped the hot tea appreciatively and warmed her old, cold hands on the glass.

Pat was happy to see her take several cookies. "The check should be here soon."

Olga nodded. "That is why I come." She slowly opened her worn, brown leather pocketbook, reached in with shaky fingers and withdrew a small blue booklet. Handing it to Pat, she said, "You put in for me."

Pat was momentarily saddened. It was tough to get old. Olga must really be feeling weak if she was handing over her bank savings passbook. The elderly Russian lady was adamant about taking care of her banking herself. Though Pat had volunteered to make trips to Westwood Savings Bank for her, Olga had always declined. Life experience had taught Olga to guard her monies carefully, and she had always wanted to see the deposits made herself.

"Okay, Olga. I'll be glad to take care of it. I'll deposit the check as soon as it arrives and then I'll drop the passbook off at your apartment."

"Good. My Papa, he take care of me again." Olga delicately worked on her short-bread cookie. "How is my Peter?" she asked, changing the subject.

Pat smiled broadly. "Wonderful. He's loving college and, thanks to you, he is most enthusiastic about the course on Russian history he's taking this semester."

"He is good boy."

"Yes, Olga, he is."

Of anything in her life, Pat was most proud of Peter. Her son, her only child. It seemed like such a short time ago that she had watched him ride his tricycle down the driveway, and wondered how he was going to make it without his father. But over the years, the two of them had depended on each other. As a single mother she had worked hard at raising him and at starting her own business. He had worked hard at school and tried to help his mother by not giving her much to worry about. Pat was grateful that in an age of horror stories about drug and alcohol abuse, as far as she knew, the worst Peter had pulled was smoking in the Westwood High men's room. He'd been mortified when he was caught, and she'd been called to school for a conference with the principal. Afterward, contrite and very upset, Peter promised Pat that he wouldn't do it again. His mother believed him.

Since he had first started going to school, Peter would come to the Consignment Depot at the end of the schoolday. She could still remember watching the little redheaded boy swinging his book bag as he skipped up the sidewalk. Some days her heart felt as if it would literally burst with the love she felt for her child. He'd always be so happy to see his mother, giving her a big, hard hug. He would eagerly head for the kitchen for an after-school snack, and then he'd tell her the details of his day, what his teacher had said, who got yelled at, who had gotten into fights in the schoolyard. For Pat, the best part of having her own business was that it had allowed her to be there for her son after school each day.

Peter had been in the shop when, years

ago, Olga had brought in her first piece of Fabergé, a silver letter opener. Not understanding the concept of a consignment shop, Olga had wanted Pat to buy the letter opener. Patiently Pat had explained that she didn't buy things, she only displayed and sold them for other people. Upon scrutinizing the silver piece, Pat had checked a book out of the public library and correctly identified the Cyrillic markings on it to read "Fabergé." Pat let Olga know that the piece was probably too valuable to get the right kind of customer exposure in the Consignment Depot anyway. She urged Olga to take it to New York. Somehow, in her halting but persuasive English, the old lady had convinced Pat to go to New York for her.

Pat had shown the letter opener with its famous markings to her son. She explained the history of the wondrous House of Fabergé and the connection with the doomed Romanov dynasty. Peter was enthralled, later choosing to do a term paper on the Russian Revolution. As part of his research, he decided to approach the old Russian lady and see if she could give him some first hand stories of that historic time.

Olga came to love Peter. At first hesitantly,

then more and more openly, she told the young man stories of her early life, and ways of the Old Country. Even after the school assignment was completed, Peter kept going over to see the old lady once a week. She complimented him on his name. "Peter the Great was the father of all Russia. Your name is strong. You be strong man, too." Peter's love for Russian history was born.

But now, turning over the blue passbook in her hands, Pat's thoughts turned from her son back to the Russian woman.

"Olga, what will you do after this money is gone?" she asked gently.

"Don't worry," she answered in a surprisingly firm voice. "I still have one thing left."

✂ Chapter 19

"It's not working out, is it?"

Farrell sat before Range Bullock, and though the door to the office was closed, a sign that the executive producer did not want any interruptions, Farrell knew she was on display for all the newsroom to see. The glass wall that fronted the newsroom was an invitation to gawk at the players inside the Fishbowl. She tried to arrange the expression on her face. Don't let Bullock or any of the voracious busybodies posted in the newsroom see the panic she felt inside. Look confident, or they'll smell blood.

She'd made one last trip to the ladies' room in another attempt to blot out the coffee stain on her shirt, but her rubbing had only made it worse. She saw Range glance at the brown spot on the snow-white field of her blouse, and she supposed her sloppiness would only be another nail in the coffin of Range's opinion of her. She crossed her legs.

As usual, Farrell had felt it necessary to talk first. Why? She remembered the old saying, *He who talks first, loses*. But it was her nature to take things head-on. Most times she liked that about herself. But this time, she should have let Range talk first. Let him bring up the tough subject. Put the ball in his court. Instead, Farrell had served right to him and she sensed his relief.

"We missed a good story last night," Range responded ruefully.

"We didn't *miss* it. A decision was *made* not to do it." Farrell left unspoken the *made by you, Range.*

For a moment Range glared at her, but when he spoke again, he sounded more resigned than angry.

"You're right, Farrell. I did decide not to go with it and now I'm sorry. I misjudged. I take full responsibility for that."

Farrell sat quietly, waiting for him to continue.

Range rose and walked around his desk, taking a seat beside Farrell on the other end of the gray tweed couch. He angled his body toward her and bent forward, staring at his hands.

"Look, I want to be honest here."

"Please do."

"In my thirty years of working in this business, I've learned to trust my instincts. My instincts are telling me that I shouldn't renew your contract."

Farrell had known it was coming. Why, she wondered, did she feel the wind knocked out of her when it actually happened? A blow to the solar plexus. She inhaled deeply, but she'd be damned if she would cry. She dug her nails into her thigh.

"Don't you think you should base such an important decision on fact rather than instinct?"

Farrell thought she detected a tinge of admiration in Bullock's eyes. He seemed to consider her question.

"You're right. True, your work is basically solid. There hasn't been a story I can point to and say, 'See, Farrell screwed up. She made mistakes, she left out something important.' But you haven't been aggressive, either. I don't see you going after stories, pursuing them vigorously. You don't seem sold on your own work. Case in point, the Fabergé auction."

"Hey, I told you we should do that story," Farrell protested.

"Barely. You expressed no enthusiasm or commitment, no hunger. You could have sold me on it and you didn't. In fact, sometimes I sense you're almost relieved not to have to do a piece."

Farrell snapped. "If there's any truth in that, it's only because I know that you won't go for anything involving me. The cards are stacked against me in the first place."

Range opened his mouth to say something, but stopped. He rose and walked back behind his desk.'

"Well, then, perhaps we should write it off to bad chemistry," he said coolly. "And that is a good enough reason for me. The *Evening Headlines* producers are part of a very well-trained, exclusive team. We have to play well together, anticipate and under-stand each other."

"So. . . ." She trailed off. She was going to make him say it.

"Your contract expires in six weeks. It won't be renewed. You better start looking for another job."

Farrell skulked back to her office, Range's dictum pounding in her head. In a funny way, she was relieved. At least it was out on the table.

What was she going to do now? She should start making some phone calls right away, start sniffing around to see what was out there. She had connections at the other networks.

What was she going to answer when asked why she was leaving KEY News? She could say that after working at the net-work for fifteen years, she'd wanted to try someplace new, start something fresh, didn't want to get stale. They might buy that.

Or she could just tell the truth. She hadn't gotten along with her executive producer. Just about everyone in the industry had, at one time or another, an executive producer he clashed with. Personality conflicts were de rigueur in the television news business.

She supposed she might as well go with the truth. Whoever might interview her at the new place could easily pick up the phone and call Range. No point in lying when they would just find out the truth anyway.

Ugh. Looking for a job. The worst. Farrell marveled that some people actually liked it, enjoyed the search, the challenge of the hunt for better employment. She despised it.

But that could be symptomatic of the bigger problem. She hated to admit to herself that Range could have a point. Maybe she *wasn't* hungry enough. Why hadn't she insisted more strenuously about the Fabergé story?

The hallway leading to her office was deserted. She prayed that her office would be empty as well. The last thing she wanted to deal with now was Dean Cohen.

No such luck.

Dean was putting on his coat to go home.

If only she'd been a minute later, she'd have missed him entirely.

Don't look upset, she commanded herself.

"Everything okay?" Dean looked concerned.

Was he sincere? Maybe. But she didn't want to go into it with him.

"Yup. Everything's fine. Just fine."

Chapter 20

Sticky. That much blood was sticky. Despite the rubber gloves, despite the slicker and galoshes, despite the goggles and the cap, Misha's blood found a way to ooze through the plastic, the plasma tacky and thick.

How did those guys in the meatpacking industry do it? Perhaps if you did it enough, it got easier, maybe you got used to it—hacking and sawing your way through skin and muscle, sinew and bones.

And the sound. That was the worst part of all. Joints snapped and popped. Bones broke with a sickening crack. And the saw droned steadily, back and forth, back and forth.

Piece by piece, section by section, Misha went into black heavy-plastic garbage bags. The body was dumped in a local landfill. The head was thrown into the Hudson River along with the fingertips, food for the fish newly returned to the cleaned-up waterway. All part of the plan.

It was filthy work, and exhausting. Funny how a human being could sleep so well after so gruesome an experience. It was the sleep of the deadly . . . and the desperate—

What an idiot! In the haste of disposing of Misha, one loose end had been left dangling. The design plans—they were still out there in Little Odessa.

Chapter 21

The bony fingers of Nadine Paradise rubbed the milky enamel crescent she'd bought at the Churchill's auction. Her eyes, eyes that had watched vigilantly for nearly eight decades, appreciatively took in every detail of the work of art that was meant to be worn.

Life was strange. After eight decades on this earth, she knew this. That she should now own both halves of the brooch, proved it.

There were some things she should cut back on, but the purchase of this pin was a necessity, not a luxury.

Nadine sighed and sat back in the comfortably worn, green velvet armchair, her old eyes falling on the silver-framed black-and-white picture sitting on the mahogany table beside her. A young ballerina in a feathered headpiece was caught in midair in one of a series of whipping turns from *Swan Lake*. Nadine remembered with pleasure that the most famous ballet critic of the time had called her dancing both "astonishing" and "frightening."

The former prima ballerina closed her eyes, remembering how she and her mother had painstakingly inspected the stage to choose the exact spot at which Nadine would perform those notoriously difficult turns known as pirouettes. They prayed over the spot. Nadine's pirouettes never faltered.

Mother. Nadine's fiercest partisan and sternest critic. What a life she'd led. Raising a child alone in Paris after the Revolution, struggling to find a way to let her dark-haired Nadine study the dance.

Over the years, mother had accompanied daughter as she toured the world. Acting as dresser, laundress, cook, and chaperone, Mother had loved to play poker, believed in fortune-telling, faith-healing and, most of all, in Nadine.

"I didn't disappoint you, Mother." Nadine murmured the words aloud. It was a distinguished career. Dancing first with the Ballet Russe, followed by the American Ballet Theater for Balanchine, then dancing and acting in several motion pictures, and then, in an ironic turn of events, marriage to a man who had brought her back to Russia as the wife of a diplomat.

She'd been unable to have children of her own. But they'd adopted a beautiful Russian child. Victor. She wished her grown son was as smart as he was good-looking.

Nadine's had been an interesting life, and though she was all too aware that she was in its final act, she felt an excitement as she held both halves of the crescent brooch. It had been a long time since she'd felt this way.

Life, even at this stage, continued to surprise. There was satisfaction in the knowledge that things eventually did come around, if one waited long enough.

Nadine knew who had owned the jeweled pin and believed the possessor to be long dead. But perhaps he wasn't. Perhaps her father was still alive!

No, that couldn't be. Her father would be over a hundred years old.

She rose from her chair and walked to the antique walnut secretary. Opening the paneled doors at the top, she felt beneath the shelf for the button. Pushing it, a small concealed drawer on the side of the secretary slid open. Nadine felt among the contents and gingerly lifted a small packet of letters, yellowed and flaking with age.

Yet again, she began to read the fading Cyrillic script.

My darling Nadjia . . .

The days pass—slowly, achingly, and I long for you, my dearest one.

Why did you go? How could you leave me?

And yet I know the answer. St. Petersburg is a bitter, living hell and you were right to get out when you had the chance.

Oh, my Nadjia, how I wish we were together. And how I pray we will be reunited someday.

Until then, my darling, wear this pin. . . . I designed and executed it myself. . . . A big, round moon . . . of enamel and sapphires. Each month, when the moon is full, look up at the vast dark sky and wish upon it. Hope and wish and pray that we will soon be together again.

Know, Nadjia, that I will be here in Russia . . . looking up, too. I have another pin, a companion piece to yours. Mine is the moon, too, but in its crescent phase. And I will be wishing on the slivered moon.

Between us, the moon is ours, in its wax-
ing and its waning. And when we are to-
gether again, we will slip the moons
together, a masterpiece to behold.
My love to you for all eternity,
'V.'

Nadine removed the round enamel-and-
sapphire pin she had worn almost every day
since her mother Nadjia had died. As she
lay dying, mother had given daughter the
round pin as she whispered the story of her
true love, Nadine's father. She had passed
away before telling her daughter her father's
name.

Now, as she fitted the round moon to her
newly acquired crescent, Nadine trembled
as she realized that the two pieces did in-
deed create a masterpiece.

The round, full moon, joined to its crescent, together formed an oval—a miniature
Moon Egg.

Chapter 22

Maybe she should think about a whole new career. Flipping hamburgers at McDonald's looked real good right now. You worked your shift and went home. No mind games.

Farrell stood in the tiny galley kitchen of her West Side apartment and twisted the can opener.

"C'mon, Walter. Here, Jane." She put two small ceramic bowls on the floor, one red and one blue. In true anchor style, Walter Cronkat and Jane Pawley didn't share. The cats each demanded, and got, their own.

Four years at Sarah Lawrence, graduating at the top of her class, fifteen years at KEY News, the pinnacle of broadcast journalism, multiple Emmys, and hundreds of thousands of miles logged covering fascinating stories, and now *this*.

What do I have to show for all of it? she asked herself, glancing at the awards collecting dust on the crowded bookcase.

Her personal life was empty.

She thought of Rick and wondered what might have been. What if she had followed him to Atlanta when he had taken the job with CNN? At the time, they had thought a long-distance relationship could work out. How naive they had been.

Now Rick was married to someone else, with a second baby on the way. And Farrell doubted she would ever have a child.

Thursday night, and the March weekend loomed gray and long. Farrell's mind was reeling. The thought of looking for another job depressed her—big time. Nor did she want to dwell on Range's words—or worse, consider that he might be right. Maybe she *wasn't* aggressive enough, hadn't gotten psyched enough about her stories. She had to admit that sometimes she found herself just going through the motions at work. And that wasn't good enough.

Procrastination was always an option. She didn't want to spend the weekend analyzing herself and thinking about her uncertain future. She could call Robbie. But the idea held little solace for her. In the sibling relationship they had, Farrell, as the older of the two, was the comforter. She did not think going to Robbie would make her feel better. She would feel guilty leaning on him when, in her opinion, he could barely take care of himself.

Farrell wanted to get away. She should get out of the city. A change of scenery, that's what she needed. But where?

Someplace close by, but a world away from KEY News.

Chapter 23

Olga lit a fresh white candle beneath the icon of the Virgin and Child that hung in the *krasny ugol*, the beautiful corner of her tiny living room. She closed her eyes and prayed, as she always did.

"Holy Mother, forgive us. Holy Mother, protect us. Holy Mother, pray for us."

The frail old woman reached up to smooth the linen stole that draped the gold-rimmed icon. It was a white scarf on which, so many years ago, she had carefully stitched tiny birds, flowers, and trees with bright red threads. Then, she had been a young girl with good eyes. That was before she had escaped from Russia; before she made it to America.

The embroidery was one of the few things she'd been able to take with her. She'd used it to wrap up the exquisite pieces of Fabergé.

The Fabergé. Pat had gotten seven thousand dollars for the brooch. That should hold for a while. It had to. With the crescent brooch gone, there was only one piece of Fabergé left.

Potted red begonias lined the windowsill, and Olga decided they needed to be watered. She went to the kitchenette sink, filled a glass with water, and shuffled slowly to the flowers. Olga tended her plants lovingly and she had gotten years of enjoyment from these particular begonias. Especially in the winter, in the gray, dark months, the flowers cheered her.

Olga lived carefully, frugally, and that was fine by her. It was all she had ever known, really. Life was hard, Olga knew that. But she was one of the lucky ones. America was her country. In Russia, she was scared all the time. In America she was free and she didn't live in fear.

Except about the Fabergé.

Chapter 24

Grateful for the increased physical strength she'd developed since she'd been working out, Pat easily moved a walnut writing desk to a spot where it would be shown to greater advantage in the Consignment Depot living room, when a sudden blast of winter air from the opened front door signaled the arrival of Stacey Spinner. Stacey, the owner of Spun Gold Interiors, stopped at the Depot at least once a week, always on the prowl for anything new that came into the shop.

Pat knew that Stacey's interior design business was thriving. Saddle River was only a few miles but a world apart from Westwood and the Consignment Depot. Spun Gold Interiors by Stacey Spinner catered to people who had too much money and too little time. Her clients often lacked the inclination or the confidence to decorate their multimillion-dollar homes. Stacey possessed both qualities in abundance. Pat knew that Stacey bought things at the Consignment Depot and then turned around and sold them to her wealthy clients for many times what she had paid. The clients oohed and aahed about Stacey's "wonderful finds." Pat supposed that Stacey's business was a case study of capitalism in action. Hey, everyone has to make a living.

As usual, Stacey looked terrific. Though not really a pretty woman, she was ever so highly maintained. Her ash-blond hair was expensively cut and blown dry, her makeup expertly applied, her nails freshly manicured. (Pat had always suspected reconstructive surgery.) Her snug-fitting jeans were carefully ironed and creased precisely down the front. She wore ostrich-skin cowboy boots and a sheepskin jacket the same oatmeal color as her boots.

Pat smoothed back her own hair, and tucked in the back of her dark blue turtleneck, which had come loose from her khakis as she'd moved the desk.

"Hello, Stacey. How are you?" Pat asked politely.

"Can't complain, Pat. My business is amazing. How are things for you?"

"Well, spring fever and the urge to either clean up or perk up the home hasn't begun yet, so it's just a little slow. But we did get in a few interesting things this week. Take a look around."

Pat watched as Stacey's radar zeroed in immediately on the large china pot that had come in two days ago. Decorated with showy peonies in graduated shades from palest to brightest pinks, the pot was a Chinese export and dated from the late 1800s.

"Where did this come from?" Stacey asked, as if she had only a mild interest. But Pat knew from experience that the feigned lack of enthusiasm really meant Stacey would be taking out her Gucci-covered checkbook.

"A local family was cleaning out the estate of an elderly aunt."

Stacey checked the price tag.

"Four hundred? Isn't that a little steep?"

"It's worth it, Stacey."

The decorator moved on through the shop without committing to the Chinese pot, but

once the front door opened again and another customer arrived, Stacey made a bee-
line back to her treasure.

"I'll take it."

As Stacey made out her check to the Consignment Depot, she told Pat, "Don't forget
to give me a call if anything else good
comes in from that estate."

 Chapter 25

The new BMW sedan pulled into the circular
drive in front of the stately Tudor mansion.
As the driver switched off the ignition, she
made the wish she made each and every
time she arrived at Nadine Paradise's home.
God, I wish this house was mine. But unlike
so many wishes that people make, Stacey
Spinner knew her wish had a very good
chance of coming true.

After her trip to the Consignment Depot
she had gone home to change, and then
headed right to the beautiful old home.

Stacey swung her jodhpur-clad legs out of

the car, her shiny leather riding boots sinking into the crushed-stone covered driveway. Those legs had never known actual contact with a horse, but the equestrian look was meant to look elegantly casual. Everything Stacey did was painstakingly calculated.

Carefully she lifted the large Chinese porcelain pot from the backseat and, holding it close, made her way up the wide fieldstone steps that led to the heavy double doors. Nadine Paradise herself answered the bell.

"Mrs. Paradise! As always, so good to see you. You're looking so well!" Stacey eyed the brooch anchored to Nadine's charcoal-gray cashmere dress. "What a beautiful pin!"

Nadine's thin arms reached up and her fingers delicately rubbed the brooch. The crescent of enamel and sapphires preened upon the dark soft wool.

"Thank you, Stacey. Won't you come in?"

Stacey entered the spacious entry hall, careful to appear nonchalant in the elegant surroundings. Her boots clicked on the marble floor as she caught a look at herself in the enormous, ornate gilded mirror that hung from the mahogany wall. Briefly she imagined herself to be the lady of the house, home from a day of antiquing.

"I've been looking forward to seeing this," Nadine said eagerly, reaching for the porcelain pot in Stacey's arms. "Even though I really shouldn't be buying anything," she added.

"It's very heavy, Mrs. Paradise. Let me put it down on the table in the conservatory so you can have a good look at it. The colors are just perfect for the room. I thought it might look wonderful with your orchids growing from it."

As the two women walked across the fine old Oriental rugs on their way to the conservatory, Nadine complimented her interior decorator.

"Stacey, I know why you are so successful. You make your clients feel that you love and care about their homes as much as they do."

Not their *homes, Mrs. Paradise. It's just* your *home I really love.*

Chapter 26

Jackie Kennedy boosted Sotheby's, Princess Diana advanced Christie's, and now, thank God, the romance and history of Fabergé was helping Churchill's, Clifford Montgomery thought to himself, with a mixture of pleasure and relief. He checked the New York Stock Exchange listings in the *Wall Street Journal.* Churchill's stock had gained three points since the announcement of the sale.

In the president's office, Clifford sat back in his red leather chair, momentarily relishing the knowledge that he held options for more than one hundred thousand shares of the auction house's stock. For him, every quarter-point equaled twenty-five thousand dollars—every point rise, another one hundred thousand dollars. If the stock jumped ten points, Clifford would be one million dollars richer—at least on paper.

All the publicity surrounding the sale of the

Moon Egg had been a fantastic perk-up for business. Though the Wall Street professionals thought that the price-earnings ratio was too high, the public didn't seem to share their concerns. The market was always susceptible to emotions, and the history of the Moon Egg had captured the imaginations of investors. If the stock sustained its current rise, Clifford stood to become a very wealthy man.

Clifford shuddered slightly, remembering how upset Churchill's board of directors had been when Caroline and John ultimately had chosen Sotheby's for the sale of their mother's possessions. But that upset had turned to rage when that sale turned into the media event of the decade, with resulting sales of over thirty-four million dollars—so much more than Sotheby's highest estimates.

The next year, Princess Diana had selected Christie's to sell seventy-nine of her dresses because she wanted to raise money for cancer and AIDS research. Three-and-a-quarter million in sales, and priceless goodwill and publicity for Christie's.

Clifford stroked his dark, bearded chin, remembering that miserable time. To add insult to injury, Churchill's had experienced a severe downturn in business after each of those sales. Those with estates to dispose of, or treasures they wanted to sell, chose Sotheby's or Christie's, not Churchill's. They liked thinking their things were being sold by the same people who were good enough for England's princess and America's queen.

It was a vicious circle. The choicest merchandise was consistently consigned to the competition, and that merchandise drew better crowds of bidders, which drew higher prices and more publicity. Churchill's was drowning. Clifford sensed that he was very close to losing his job. As the only African-American to rise to the presidency of a major auction house, he knew that his every move was under the microscope. He didn't want to fail.

Then, a lifeline—Churchill's chance to auction the fabled Moon Egg. Clifford had seized the opportunity hungrily, and capitalized on it by scheduling the auction at the same time the long-anticipated "Riches of Russia's Romanovs" exhibit was being featured at the Metropolitan Museum of Art. After viewing the Russian treasures at the

Met, those with the means and inclination could buy their own souvenir of Russian history and culture around the corner at Churchill's. To keep the excitement going, Churchill's would be featuring auctions with Russian themes all month.

A knock at the office door interrupted Clifford's reverie. Meryl Quan entered, carrying her ever-present clipboard. Now only twenty-four, Meryl had graduated from Vanderbilt University with a fine-arts degree, then packed herself off to London to enroll in Sotheby's Works of Art course. For the next nine months, she'd immersed herself in the study of paintings and decorative art. When she'd moved to New York, she'd found her first paying job as a floater at Churchill's.

Meryl tackled the entry-level job enthusiastically, working the floor, answering telephones, doing whatever anyone asked of her. With her keen mind and positive attitude, she impressed everyone she worked for. When it came time to choose another assistant, there had been general agreement that Meryl Quan, though young, should get the position.

Clifford regarded the woman. Her shiny

black hair glowed in the sunlight that streamed through the office window overlooking Madison Avenue. Her dark eyes peered from almond-shaped openings. Clear, smooth skin; straight nose; even, white teeth behind a delicately shaped mouth. All that and brains, too.

God, I wouldn't be surprised if she had my job one day.

"Nadine Paradise called. She wants to know more about the brooch she bought at the Fabergé auction."

Meryl Quan was eager to go over details of the sale with Clifford Montgomery. Clifford half listened, a smile of satisfaction on his face as he perused the rest of the *Journal.*

"That was the enamel-and-sapphire crescent pin, wasn't it?"

Meryl nodded. She admired Clifford's file-cabinet mind. It amazed her how well he could recall the buyers and sellers of so many of the items auctioned off at Churchill's. But then again, Nadine Paradise was a very good customer. Not only had she bought often over the years, the legendary prima ballerina also had name recognition. Churchill's liked having a star-studded salesroom.

"What does she want to know?" he sighed, reluctantly folding up the newspaper.

Meryl had been observing Clifford closely over the last months and wondered if her boss would be happier working on Wall Street than he was managing a major auction house. Clifford was constantly reading the *Times'* business section, *Baron's*, and the *Wall Street Journal*, and watching CNBC on the small television set in his office. She'd never seen Clifford excited until the day a CNBC reporter came to interview him for a piece on the competition among Sotheby's, Christie's, and Churchill's.

"She wants to know who consigned the brooch."

"Pat Devereaux brought that piece in to us, didn't she?"

Again Meryl marveled at Clifford's sharp memory. Wanting to be prepared, Meryl had looked up the sales record on the crescent pin before meeting with Clifford.

"Yes," she answered. "But apparently Ms. Devereaux was acting as an agent for someone else who wished to remain anonymous."

"Did you tell Mrs. Paradise that?"

Meryl shook her head. "I thought you'd

want to explain it to her yourself, especially with her own auction coming up in three weeks."

"You're absolutely right, Meryl. Mrs. Paradise should feel that she is of utmost importance to us. I will call her myself."

❧ Chapter 27

Misha was gone. And just like in the best crimeland movies, it wasn't pretty. Blood covered almost every surface of the small apartment. Special Agent Jack McCord surveyed the mess.

Now it was too late. The crime-lab guys could dust all they wanted, but Jack knew they weren't going to come up with anything. Now he could show that idiot Quick exactly why he should have okayed the round-the-clock surveillance team. It would be fun to rub it in.

Jack studied the workbench. Like surgeon's instruments, the jeweler's tools were carefully arranged above the worktable.

With his rubber-gloved hand, Jack examined a piece that looked like a scalpel. As he turned it over, the tool slipped from his grasp, hit the linoleum floor, and slid beneath the workbench. As Jack went to retrieve it, he bumped his head on the bottom of the bench as he pulled himself to his feet. That should have hurt more, he thought to himself.

Sliding his hand along the undersurface of the table, he found taped to it a package wrapped in plastic. Jack carefully and quickly unfastened it and slipped it into his jacket pocket.

Chapter 28

Pat was surprised when Farrell called to say she wanted to come for a visit. Until that day at Churchill's they'd completely lost touch with one another.

Pat replaced the receiver in the cradle.

The last time she'd seen Farrell, Peter had been a baby. It was Christmastime. Farrell, then a college sophomore, had brought over a tiny Santa Claus sleeper for Peter, complete with a little red pointed cap.

They'd dressed Peter up in it, and they'd had a good laugh and agreed that he was probably the cutest baby in the whole world.

But after that, it had been awkward, as their lives went off in different directions. Pat felt that Farrell thought she was stupid to be married and a mother at such a young age. Farrell's talk about what was going on at school was as alien to Pat as chatter about baby teeth was to her friend. By the end of the afternoon visit, both young women were edgy and uncomfortable.

Neither one had followed up after that.

How stupid we were! Pat thought to herself. But her life had been so busy. And the years had just passed.

After Allan's death, Pat heard that Mr. and Mrs. Slater had sold their house on O'Toole Street and moved to a condominium in Sarasota, Florida. She'd assumed that there wasn't much reason for Farrell to come back to Westwood anymore.

From time to time, Pat had thought about her old friend and wondered what had become of her.

What would Farrell think of Pat's small-town, humdrum existence compared to the exciting life a KEY News producer must lead?

Chapter 29

Saturday

Farrell couldn't remember the last time she'd taken a bus anywhere, much less out to Westwood. Since her parents had moved to Florida, there had been no reason to return to her hometown. She'd completely lost track of her friends from grammar school and high school. Only occasionally, she'd get together with college friends, meeting in the city somewhere for drinks and dinner. But she feared she had become pretty one-dimensional. Work was the main focus of Farrell's life. Big mistake. Because when work went south, there wasn't much to fall back on.

She was surprised at how much she was

looking forward to her visit with Pat. They had once been fast friends, walking home together day after day, leaving the nuns at St. Andrew's School behind. They'd stop at the Dinner Bell Deli, buying a couple of Cokes and splitting a package of Yankee Doodles. Cupcakes in hand, they'd make their way past the public junior high, steeling themselves for the predictable scathing comments about their navy plaid uniforms from the kids whose parents didn't force them to go to Catholic school.

They'd been in the same Girl Scouts troop, had had sleep-overs, gone to the movies, and taken what were, back then, adventurous trips by bus all the way to the Bergen Mall. Years later, Farrell could still remember Pat's parents' phone number.

But high school had split them up. Farrell's parents had insisted that she go to Immaculate Heart Academy, the all-girl prep school in the next town. Although Pat had passed the school's stringent entrance exam, and was offered acceptance, her parents hadn't had the money to pay for the tuition. It was Westwood High for Pat.

For a while, they'd continued to hang out

together. But as time passed, each girl became increasingly involved in after-school activities and made new friends at her respective school. Farrell had worked on the school paper and *Halcyon*, the IHA yearbook. For Pat, her main extracurricular activities had been cheerleading, and the good-looking Allan Devereaux.

Farrell remembered how shocked she had been when she heard that Pat was not going on to college.

"What a *waste*," she'd wailed to her mother.

"Not everyone is made for college, Farrell."

"Well, Pat *is*. She was the smartest girl in her eighth grade class! Or I thought she was. I can't believe that she isn't going to college. I heard she's going to marry Allan Devereaux instead. How can she just throw her life away?"

The red-and-tan bus pulled to a stop at the depot across the street from the flag-festooned gazebo perched in the manicured park, a picture-postcard of life in small-town America. Perhaps Pat hadn't made such a bad decision after all, Farrell thought.

🌹 Chapter 30

If Nadine Paradise was the type to give up easily, she never would have accomplished all she had done over her long, rich life. If Clifford Montgomery could not, or would not, tell her where the crescent brooch had come from, Nadine would try a different tack.

"Victor," she called.

Her adopted son appeared in the doorway of the conservatory, wearing a white polo shirt and shorts, a tennis racquet in his hand. Victor was off for another morning at the club.

"Yes, Mother?"

"Please, sit down for a minute, dear."

Victor obeyed, but Nadine knew he was anxious not to be late for his tennis game. He sat on the edge of the chair, fiddling with the strings of the racquet. She didn't know his partner, Stacey Spinner, was waiting for him. Victor didn't want her to know. She didn't have to know everything, did she?

"Victor, I need you to help me with something. I want to find out where the pin I bought at the auction with you came from. Clifford Montgomery at Churchill's says he can't tell me because the seller wishes to remain anonymous."

"Then what do you want me to do?"

"He did give me the name of the seller's agent. It turns out she has some sort of antique shop in Westwood. I would like you to go over to see her and find out who she sold the pin for."

Nadine could tell her son did not care for his assignment. Victor didn't like to be put out, even for her. She halfheartedly told herself it wasn't because he was lazy, but because he lacked self-confidence. It was safer for him not to try to accomplish anything. But how hard could this be? A shopkeeper in Westwood shouldn't be too much of a problem. Even for Victor.

"What's her name?" he asked, sighing heavily.

"Patricia Devereaux, and I would appreciate it if you would go over and speak to her *today*."

Chapter 31

Farrell entered the vestibule of the Consignment Depot and took in the shop, pleased at how welcoming it was. Pat had a real flair for displaying the objects for sale to their best advantage. Anyone walking in could not help but be drawn to the wonderful treasures that awaited.

She spotted Pat at the back of the store, talking with a customer. Pat saw Farrell at the same time, and waved. "Farrell! I'm so glad you're here. I'll be right with you."

Farrell unbuttoned her navy wool pea coat and hung it on an oak wall rack conveniently placed at the front of the shop. Adjusting her green tunic sweater down over her tan corduroys, she began slowly poking around the gleaming mahogany tables covered with artfully arranged shining sterling, sparkling cut glass, and fine crystal. Hand-stitched pillows perched on a velvet-tufted Victorian settee, delicate lacework draped a cherry card table with ball-and-claw feet. A gold-leafed, pagoda-crowned Chinese Chippendale mirror hung over the old fireplace mantel, lighted candles reflecting in its glass.

Farrell thought of her own apartment and how she had neglected it. She still had most of her books in cardboard boxes stacked against a living-room wall because she used her bookcase as a catchall for junk. Her sofa was a hand-me-down from her parents' housecleaning when they had made their move to Florida. She'd never really liked it, but she hadn't managed to do anything about it. The same was true for the table and chairs in her dining area. She'd barely bothered to hang anything on the walls, and what was there, was haphazardly arranged. A bulletin board, tacked with souvenirs, press releases, and newspaper clippings about favorite stories she'd worked on, belonged more in her office at KEY or in a college student's dorm than in the living room of a Manhattan apartment of a woman who— ugh, she hated to admit it—was pushing forty.

Pat had finished her conversation with the customer, and came toward Farrell with open arms. "It's so good to see you!" she said warmly, embracing Farrell in a big hug.

"What a terrific place!" Farrell gestured sweepingly. "I am so impressed. Do you make house calls?"

Pat laughed. "I'm so glad you like it. I have to admit, I've been a little nervous about your coming and what you would think about my little shop. It must seem so small-time to you."

"Honey, you couldn't be more wrong."

✤ Chapter 32

Peter watched as Charlie made three thick turkey sandwiches. "Heavy on the mayo on mine, Charlie."

"Why three sandwiches today, Peter?" asked Charlie, as he sliced a pale-looking tomato.

"Mom has an old friend visiting."

"Oh yeah? Who?"

"Someone she went to school with a million years ago. She seems pretty cool. She's a producer for KEY News."

Charlie nodded as he cut the sandwiches and wrapped them in white paper. "Chips?"

"Mmm. Barbecue. And a Coke and two coffees."

The deli owner packed a brown sack with the Consignment Depot lunch order. "You know, Peter, you're a good kid. Coming up here every Saturday to help your mom. Most kids wouldn't be bothered."

Peter thought about it a minute. "Yeah, I guess so. But it's been just Mom and me for so long. And she's been such a good mother. She's really devoted her life to taking care of me. The least I can do is help her when I can."

"True. But I hope you're having a little fun, too. These are good years, Peter. College is a time for you to branch out on your own. I doubt your mom expects you to spend all your spare time with her. For example, what are you doing tonight?"

Peter looked embarrassed. "Having dinner with Mom's friend."

Charlie shook his head. "See what I mean?"

"It won't be so bad. Actually, I'm kinda looking forward to it. Farrell seems really smart and she has a great job. I'll bet she has some great stories, too. Besides, after dinner I'm going back to Seton Hall for a keg party."

"Good. That's more like it. It's the kind of thing a guy your age should be doing now, while you don't have any big responsibilities. You've got to live a little, kid. Although, don't tell your mom I said that. She wouldn't be too happy to know I'm supporting the idea of a little underage drinking."

As Peter peeled off the dollar bills to pay, Charlie asked, "How come you're having dinner with your mother's friend? Why don't just the two of them go?"

"Oh, Mom finally has a date."

Charlie felt his heart sink.

Chapter 33

"I'm very sorry, Mr. Paradise, but I can't tell you. The person who sold the crescent pin doesn't want his or her identity known." Pat was careful not to give a clue as to the sex of the seller.

The man who stood before Pat was clearly uncomfortable. He shifted from foot to foot and he'd already dropped his car keys twice on the hooked rug that covered the office area of the Consignment Depot. Stacey Spinner was with him, having explained her presence there as Nadine Paradise's decorator.

"You know, Pat, Nadine Paradise was one of the most famous ballerinas in the world."

"Sure, Stacey, even I, buried here in little old Westwood, have heard of Nadine Paradise." *Don't try so hard to impress, Stacey,* Pat said to herself.

"My mother *bought* the pin," he pleaded.

"She paid a good deal of money for it. She really wants to know where it came from."

"Come on, Pat, I can vouch for Victor." Stacey entwined her fingers in his and batted her baby-blues up at him. *So that was it,* Pat thought. Stacey had her hat set for the beefy hulk. No accounting for taste.

A reference from Stacey wasn't worth all that much to Pat. And it was somewhat distasteful to watch the interior decorator playing up to this guy. He was plainly loving it. Dope.

Pat smiled sadly and shrugged. "I wish I could help you out. But the seller insists on anonymity. I have to respect that."

The implication was clear. *You, Mr. Paradise, should respect that, too.*

But the man wasn't giving up easily.

"Isn't there anything you can do?" he appealed. "My mother will be so disappointed."

Pat was firm.

"I'm sorry."

Farrell had been busying herself inspecting an ornate wrought-iron side table, but had listened to the whole conversation. When the annoyed couple left the shop, she looked at Pat expectantly.

"Who were *they?*"

"I don't know much about him, except that his mother is Nadine Paradise. From the looks of him, that's his only claim to fame."

"And her?" Farrell asked.

Pat shook her head in disgust. "Stacey Spinner. She plays her role as a Saddle River interior decorator a little too much for my taste. She forgets I remember her from years ago—we actually met at an evening seminar at Churchill's auction house. She was working as a department-store salesgirl at the time, but smart enough to know that there was a big world out there that she wanted a part of."

Pat stopped to consider a moment.

"I've got to give Stacey credit, though. She's really built a solid business for herself and, from what I've seen and heard, she does have a certain flair. She knew what she wanted and she went for it. I admire that."

Chapter 34

Olga struggled to lift the heavy carton of Epsom salts and place it in the small wire shopping cart. It would feel good later to fill the old porcelain bathtub with the salts and hot water and sit in the soothing pool. Her arthritis was really aching today.

Slowly she finished her shopping in the aisles of CVS. A box of tissues, some soap powder, a package of butterscotch. She made her way to the cash register at the front of the store.

She waited quietly in line, waiting for her turn to pay. She watched a child cry to his mother for a Milky Way. The mother gave in.

Olga turned her head away from the spoiled child and his weak mother.

And then she saw it. Featured on the counter for the world to see.

On the cover of an American magazine, the Moon Egg glared.

The teenaged girl at the checkout counter watched as the old lady pointed in the direction of the magazines and crumpled to the floor. Instant hubbub ensued as the other customers on line and browsing near the front of the store, gawked and gasped. A strong-looking man bent over the fainted woman, rubbing her hand and talking to her.

For a few minutes, the white-haired woman lay motionless on the pharmacy floor. Then, as she began to come to, she was mumbling.

"Ma ijtso, ma ijtso."

"What's she saying?" a blond-haired woman asked, as her four-year-old tugged at her arm.

"I hope she hasn't broken a hip," another woman said with some alarm.

"Ma ijtso."

Olga's eyes opened and began to dart around, frightened.

"It's all right," said the man who bent over her. "It's all right. You just had a fainting spell."

Olga struggled to get up on her feet. She held tight to the man's arm as she tried to regain her equilibrium.

"Thank you, mister. Thank you."

"Is there someone I can call for you?" he asked.

"No. No one. I am all right in a little while."

"Do you live far from here?"

"Just a few blocks."

"Then, please, let me take you home. You shouldn't walk home by yourself."

Chapter 35

Before closing for the evening, Charlie took the pink ham from the shiny glass display case and shaved off a generous portion. He filled three plastic containers, spooning in creamy potato salad, pickled beets, and rice pudding. He packed everything up in a brown paper bag, along with a couple of seeded rolls.

He switched off the store lights and locked up. Standing out on the sidewalk in front of the delicatessen, Charlie didn't have much to look forward to in the night ahead. Maybe he'd stop on the way home and rent a video.

As he walked in the chilly evening air toward the garden apartments, he realized how much it bothered him that Pat had a date tonight . . . a date *not* with him. He'd be home, sitting in front of the television, and she'd be out with someone else.

Well, it was his own fault, wasn't it? He never got up the courage to ask her out for dinner and a movie. He'd watched her for years, admired her, dreamed about her. But he did nothing about it. Nothing to move his dream toward reality.

So here he was, good old Charlie. Dropping off some food to the elderly on Saturday night.

He knocked on Olga's apartment door and waited. He could hear the faint sound of her slow, shuffling progress to the front door.

"Who is there?"

"It's Charlie, Olga."

He heard the lock slide open as Olga unbolted the door. The diminutive woman's old face smiled with pleasure and anticipation at the sight of Charlie and his package.

"Ah, Charlie. I not know you coming tonight. You good man. So kind to think of Olga all the time."

As Charlie reached out to hand the paper

bag to Olga, he looked over her head into the apartment. Before Olga closed the door, Charlie caught a glimpse of something gleaming on the table behind her.

Chapter 36

Pat noticed that she was taking too much time trying to decide what to wear.

Six dresses were strewn across the gaily-flowered quilt on her antique iron-and-brass bed, and five pair of shoes were arrayed on the floor.

It's just dinner, for God's sake. What's the big deal?

When Tim Kavanagh called asking if she'd like to have dinner, she'd only hesitated a moment before saying yes. It had surprised her how much she'd been anticipating the evening all week. Most times she found herself dreading new dates.

Not that there really had been that many of them. She knew that she didn't give out the signals that said "approachable" and "available." Truth to tell, she usually didn't want to get involved. It was simpler that way, which translated into "safer that way."

But it felt different this time. Pat laughed to herself. *You idiot! What makes you think you are exempt from the natural human desire for the companionship of the opposite sex? Admit it. You've missed it for a long time. Too long.*

She'd narrowed the selection down to her black wool long-sleeved dress or her blue velvet cocktail dress. The black was always safe. She could dress it up with her pearl earrings and necklace.

But the velvet was more sensuous and, frankly, sexier. It hugged her well-exercised figure. When she wore it, she felt decidedly more feminine.

Go for it.

On went the velvet. She fastened on rhinestone earrings but chose to wear nothing at the open neckline. She slipped on black suede high-heeled pumps over her sheer dark hose. As Pat turned before the full length mirror, she felt confident about her appearance.

Farrell and Peter applauded when she came out of her bedroom.

"What a bod, Pat! You look fabulous," exclaimed Farrell. "You make me want to get right to the gym."

"Okay, you two. Thanks for the compliments to this nervous mother going out on a date for the first time in a long while. Farrell, you're sure this is okay?"

"Of course it is. *You're* the one doing me a favor, having me out for the weekend after I invited myself. I'd feel terrible if you canceled your date. Go, have a good time. Peter and I will have a little dinner and then I'll let him get back to Seton Hall where he should be on a Saturday night."

Pat went out into the cold March night and slid into the front seat of her eight-year-old Volvo. Tim had wanted to pick her up, but she'd insisted on meeting him at the restaurant. She always felt safer when she had her own car.

She drove the thirty miles into Manhattan and miraculously found a parking spot on West 58th Street, a half-block from her destination.

Tiny, twinkling white lights glittered, framing the entrance to Petrossian. Even in the dark, Pat could see the architectural ornateness of the building that housed the renowned restaurant. Amid the limestone gingerbread and scrollwork, bizarre little gargoyles perched on the walls, smiling or grimacing upon the people on the sidewalk below.

You guys look like you're daring me to come inside, Pat thought as she went up the steps, where an imposing doorman awaited her. She drew a deep breath as she entered.

Inside, a small shop offered the delicacies for which Petrossian was known. Jars and tins of caviar, foie gras, and pâtés lined glass shelves, while packages of smoked salmon, sturgeon, and eel rested in glistening display cases. Truffles, Russian caramels, and vodka- and cognac-filled chocolates beckoned temptingly.

Pat looked to the right, into the restaurant, and spotted Tim Kavanagh waiting at the art deco-style bar. She saw his eyes sweep over her and she could tell by his expression as she walked toward him that he was pleased. She was glad she'd opted for the midnight-blue velvet dress.

Tim rose to greet her.

"You look wonderful," he whispered.

"Thank you." Pat felt the old tingling sensation, something she hadn't felt in a long time.

A navy-blazered gentleman guided them to their table for two. As Pat took her seat, she noticed that most of the other tables were meant for two as well. The restaurant was smaller and more intimate than she had imagined it would be.

"Pat, would you like some champagne?"

"Mmm. Perfect."

As the waiter, also attired in a navy blazer with the Petrossian insignia on his breast pocket, went to fetch the Charles Heidsieck 1985, Pat enjoyed the loveliness of the surroundings and the allure of her dinner companion. How delicious to be sitting there with a man she was drawn to. God, how she had missed it—the chemistry, the attraction.

"How did you come to love all things Russian?" she asked.

Tim thought a moment before answering. "I guess it was when I read *Nicholas and Alexandra* in high school. The whole thing about the Imperial family and the czarevitch's hemophilia and Rasputin and the overthrow and murder of the Romanovs intrigued me. Also, about the same time, I saw the old Ingrid Bergman and Yul Brynner movie *Anastasia*, about the woman who claimed she was the youngest daughter of the czar and had escaped her executioners. After that, I was hooked."

Pat smiled. "You remind me of Peter. Once he started hearing stories from Olga, an elderly Russian woman who has become a surrogate grandmother for him, he couldn't get enough."

The couple sampled Sevruga, Ossetra, and Beluga caviar, as Tim explained the differences between the Caspian Sea sturgeons that produced the tiny eggs. Pat selected a salmon with lobster sauce as her main course, while Tim chose a sea-scallop soufflé served with truffles and a pressed-caviar sauce. They sampled each other's dishes, both declaring that dinner was fabulous.

Over coffee, Tim reached for Pat's hand. "I really enjoyed myself tonight, Pat."

"I did, too. The food, the surroundings . . ." She paused. "The company."

Tim smiled. "I hope there will be more evenings like this."

"Me, too."

Chapter 37

Farrell and Peter both ordered the juicy cheeseburgers for which the Iron Horse was famous, and sat back with their drinks.

"I watched you and your mother today, Peter, and I admired you. I guess I should admit it, I'm envious."

"You—envious of *us*?" Peter laughed incredulously. "I can't believe it."

"It's true. You guys have a solid life. Your mom makes a living doing something she likes to do and she does it well. She's raised a good son, and on her own, too. That's a lot to be proud of."

Peter took a drink of his Coke.

"Well, what about you, Farrell? You've accomplished a lot—you're a television news producer."

Farrell looked at the train prints that were scattered along the wall over their table, trying to decide if she felt comfortable taking in so young a confidant. What would it hurt for the kid to hear a little about how the real world worked? "Peter, I think it *sounds* more impressive than it really is. It's a job—or, at least, it has become a job. I don't seem to have the enthusiasm I once did for it. Besides, it doesn't look like I'm going to have a place at KEY News for much longer."

Peter listened intently while Farrell told him the story of what had been going on with her career.

"The Fabergé story was just the final straw. It had been coming for a long time. I just hate to go out on such a defeated note." Farrell finished off her wine and then turned philosophical. "Hey, look at the bright side. At least I ran into you and your mother again at that auction. It was worth going for that."

The burgers arrived. As Peter poured ketchup over his railroad fries, he decided to tell Farrell about the story of Olga's Moon Egg. He'd known that something had to be done with the information. Maybe it was meant to be, that he entrust Farrell with the story. KEY News could investigate as well as the police. That way he didn't have to drag his mother into it.

Farrell listened to the story Peter told. Could she actually be getting a lead to a fascinating story from this college kid? She knew that news often came from unexpected sources, but the tale Peter was spinning for her now was so fabulous that Farrell was extremely skeptical—skeptical that the story would turn out to be true, and skeptical that she would have the good luck to have it fall right into her lap like this.

"Peter, do you think you could get Olga to let us shoot some videotape of the Moon Egg?"

Peter's eyes widened and Farrell saw the Adam's apple dip as he swallowed.

"Are you kidding? In a million years, Olga's not going to allow anyone to see the Moon Egg, much less a television crew."

"Look, Peter, it won't be a big production. Just me and my cameraman, B. J. He's a great guy. It will be very calm and we'll be as unobtrusive as possible. We can do the whole thing in a half an hour."

"She won't go for it."

"I'll need this, Peter," Farrell urged. "I'll need some proof that another, *real* Moon Egg exists. Unless, of course, you could get Olga to turn the egg over to us."

"Not a chance in hell."

Farrell grinned sheepishly. "All right, all

right. But if anyone can talk her into letting us have a glimpse of the Moon Egg, it's you, Peter."

Peter looked troubled.

"What's wrong?"

"I don't want to put Olga in any kind of danger."

Farrell's expression turned serious. "I know you don't. But the truth has a way of coming out eventually. And Olga won't be in any trouble, she hasn't done anything wrong."

"What about her taking the egg from the Fabergé studio in St. Petersburg?"

"Her father took the egg. And it was over eighty years ago. Ever hear of the statute of limitations? Who do you think is going to prosecute her anyway?"

"How 'bout the Russians?" Peter offered.

"I doubt the United States government is going to hand over a little old lady to Moscow."

Peter finished off his soda, his face brightening.

"So Olga doesn't have to be scared of going to jail?"

"I'm sure of it."

"She's sure gonna be relieved to hear that."

Chapter 38

B. J had a litmus test: Hogs and Heifers.

If a woman could deal with a night at the biker bar in the heart of the New York City meatpacking district, there was hope that she would be his type. He was past the point of progressing through the series of dinners, movies, and concerts that was the traditional dating routine. That's what he used to do to get his dates ready for the big test.

Now he got right to it. What was the point of beating around the bush? If a woman couldn't deal with Hogs and Heifers, ultimately she wasn't going to be able to deal with him. He loved the wildness of the place, its total abandon.

He watched Meryl's face. It was inscrutable. What was she thinking as they maneuvered their way past the transvestites that strutted the streets leading to the bar? Did she realize that the heavily made-up, long-legged, booted and miniskirted creatures were actually men?

A tall, thin blond approached them and arched a darkly penciled eyebrow. "Want some, honey?" asked the deep baritone.

Meryl looked up at B. J. "You really know how to impress a girl, don't you?"

Outside Hogs and Heifers, dozens of Harleys were parked, their owners openly guzzling beer on the street. Passing through the black motorcycles and the sinister-looking, black-leather-jacketed bikers, Meryl took tight hold of B. J.'s arm.

It's working already, he thought.

The couple entered the smoke-filled bar, the Allman Brothers welcoming them from the blaring sound system. Confederate flags hung on the wall. A long bar lined the left wall and, overhead, scores of bras hung from the ceiling.

B. J. checked out Meryl's reaction.

"Charming," she said sarcastically, but her dark eyes sparkled.

The female bartenders wore bikini tops and short cutoffs, with cowboy boots and hats. Through megaphones, they jeered insults at the customers who left lousy tips.

"Twenty-five cents? That's what your mother gets for making out with the sailors when the fleet's in."

There was nowhere to sit and B. J. was reminded of a packed subway train that stunk of stale beer, cigarettes, and cheap cigars.

"Two PBRs," he called to a bartender over the din.

"Wow, you're a sport, B. J.," Meryl remarked. "Pabst Blue Ribbon . . . mmm."

"Come on, Meryl," B. J. laughed. "Get with the program."

The bartender popped the tops of the two cold cans of beer and plunked them down on the bar. "Now, you gotta get three shots with that, bud." She poured three jiggers of tequila, immediately swallowing her own. B. J. followed suit and grinned at Meryl expectantly.

Without blinking, Meryl put away her shot neatly. "I thought it was illegal for bartenders to drink on the job," she related earnestly.

B. J. answered with an impish shrug of his shoulders, as if to say, *Who cares?*

"What's that over there?" She pointed. A pole with barbed wire at the top stood next to the bar.

"If you can scale to the top, you get a free shot of tequila," B. J. explained.

"Clever." Meryl took a long drink of PBR.

"Come on, Mama," the megaphone called. "Get on up here and drop that bra."

She'd heard about this place, read about it in the newspaper. A lot of young movie stars came down here to party with abandon. The bras of some of the biggest Hollywood box-office draws hung over the Hogs and Heifers bar.

"Come on, now, yo! You, China girl. Get on up there and show off what your Mama gave you."

B. J. was watching Meryl for her reaction. Her face remained passive as she tried to ignore the megaphone's demands.

The bartender wasn't giving up.

"Come on, baby, we're all friends here. Share the wealth with your friends."

Meryl chugged back the rest of her beer and resolutely placed the empty can on the bar. She hoisted herself up on the bar, and before B. J.'s admiring eyes, she began to sway in rhythm to the country-rock music. As the tempo increased, so did the gyrations of Meryl's hips and the cheering of the crowd. From beneath her black wool sweater, she wiggled free of her bra and swung it over her head to the audience's delight.

When they left Hogs and Heifers an hour later, the stench of dead meat hung in the night air, and packs of moldy bacon lay strewn before them on the sidewalk. Meryl seemed not to notice, and B. J. knew this chick had passed the test.

Chapter 39

First Sunday of Lent

It had been a long time since Farrell had been to Mass at blue-bricked St. Andrew's Church, and she found it comforting this Sunday morning. Things may be unsettled in her life right now, but the church she had gone to growing up was pretty much the same as it had always been.

Farrell crossed herself with holy water from the font at the entrance, said a silent prayer, and took a seat in a pew at the back of the church. As she rubbed and blew on her icy fingers, cold from the several-block walk from Pat's house, she looked around. Nope. The old place hadn't changed. Farrell could picture all those Sunday mornings that she and Robbie, uncomfortable in their good clothes, had been marched in by their parents. They alternately sat quietly and fidgeted, eager for Mass to end so they could get their reward at Purity Bakeshop, Farrell always getting the thick crumbcake, Robbie always choosing the chocolate creme-filled donuts.

Chocolate had been Robbie's passion even back then. Thirty years later, his breakfast of choice was Cocoa Puffs or Cocoa Krispies, cereals which he'd readily accept as lunch or dinner courses as well.

Robbie. He seemed to be doing better, Farrell thought, relieved. Maybe the worst was over. Maybe it had just been an isolated episode. She prayed so.

The purple-shrouded crucifix over the altar would stay that way until Easter Sunday. Then the cross would be uncovered, symbolic of Christ's resurrection from the dead. Six weeks. In six weeks, where would she be?

She'd better start making some plans. Get some interviews lined up. Six weeks went by awfully quickly. She didn't want to think about it. *Hey, girl, you* better *start thinking about it! Your bank account isn't any too full.*

Why hadn't she saved more? She made a good salary. Where had it all gone? What did she have to show for it?

Farrell knew the answer. She lived in New York City. It didn't come cheap.

Perhaps she should give up the city life. Move back out here, get a job on the local newspaper or go work for New Jersey Network. They'd hire her in a flash. KEY News was a great credential, if Range didn't sabotage her.

It would be much less expensive to live out here in suburbia. Rents were cheaper, she wouldn't have to spend so much on clothes or going out to eat. It would be much simpler.

But would it be boring? She'd always wanted to get out of Westwood because she thought it was dullsville. Funny how appealing it was looking now.

And, hey, things happened in the 'burbs. Look at this whole Olga thing. She wished she hadn't promised not to tell Pat. Farrell really wanted to get her take on Peter's story.

But what if Peter's account was true? What a story! A candidate for the lead on *Evening Headlines*. If she could nail this down, she could hold her head high as she left. And best of all, she'd show that son of a bitch, Range.

The priest was droning on. Farrell was paying just about as much attention to his words as she had done when the nuns had herded all her grammar-school classmates to Mass every morning of Lent to start their days off right. How she'd groaned about having to climb up the hill and sit quietly in God's house, when she'd much rather be secretly making paper dolls in the scarred wooden desk she shared at school with her artistic buddy, Laura Dail. But you wouldn't dare complain out loud. That would be like *asking* Sister Raymond to twist your ear or pull your hair.

Farrell watched to see if she saw any familiar faces as the parishioners lined up to go to Communion. She didn't, but the ones there today looked like decent, hardworking people trying to do the best they could with their situations, playing the cards life dealt them.

I guess that's all any of us can do, Farrell concluded, thinking of Pat. She'd taken a really tough blow and had carried on bravely. She was a real role model.

❧ Chapter 40

Farrell and Pat spent Sunday afternoon eating a roll of raw chocolate-chip cookie dough and poring through the books on Fabergé Pat had collected.

"When Olga brought the first piece of Fabergé into the shop, I got hooked," Pat explained. "Every time I see a new book on the subject, I buy it. Here's one I bought at Hillwood—you know, cereal heiress Marjorie Merriweather Post's estate in Washington, D.C. She was a Russophile and an avid Fabergé collector. She purchased the diamond crown that Alexandra wore at her wedding to Nicholas, as well as two Imperial Easter Eggs."

"Which ones?" asked Farrell.

"See here?" Pat pointed. "This blue monogrammed egg and the Cameo Egg. But the surprises are gone from the inside of each of them. The most valuable eggs are the ones which still have their little unexpected treasures left intact."

Farrell continued flipping through the art book, through the chapters on the history of the great house of design, and artists diagrams of the works that were carefully drawn on paper before they were made into objects of gold, enamels, and precious stones. She stopped at the chapter on the Imperial Eggs and read hungrily.

There is uncertainty about the number of Imperial Eggs produced by Fabergé. This reflects the private nature of their commission and execution. They were not considered to be created for the public's enjoyment, not to be displayed for the world to see. They were, instead, family gifts from the czar, personal tokens of his affection.

Ten eggs were made during the reign of Alexander III and another forty-four were made for Nicholas II. Two more eggs were designed and made in 1917, although they were lost and there is no evidence they were ever delivered to the czarina Alexandra or to the czar's mother, the dowager empress Marie Feodorovna, before the Romanovs were overthrown.

The Moon Egg was one of the last two eggs, Farrell thought, *ordered by the czar not knowing that he and his family would be killed within the year.* She shivered and continued reading.

The Armory Museum of the Kremlin has ten of the Imperial Eggs. America has a richer collection of the precious eggs, twelve of them at the Forbes Museum in New York City. There are a number of eggs in European collections and there are some owners who are reluctant to admit they possess Imperial Eggs, knowing their value and not wanting to explain how they came by the treasures.

Olga.
Farrell wished again she could tell Pat about Peter's story. But she had promised not to tell.

Chapter 41

Unlocking the door to her apartment and switching on the lights, Farrell backed down the little hallway that led to her living room. She held up one end of the wrought-iron side table and Pat lifted the other.

"Well, here it is." Farrell gestured widely. "Welcome to my abode. Is it everything I said it was?"

"That and more!" Pat laughed, looking around the sparsely furnished room.

"Think you can help me do anything with it?"

"Absolutely. By the time we're done, *Architectural Digest* will want to do a feature on this place." Pat took off her coat. "You game for a little moving around right now?" she asked, rubbing her hands together.

"Sure."

Pat directed and both women tugged and lifted and pushed Farrell's furniture into new positions. The forest-green leather couch slid from a side wall to the spot beneath the picture window.

"There!" said Pat, with satisfaction. "Now you can sit here with your feet up, sip your morning coffee with your newspaper, and watch the world go by on the street below."

Why didn't I think of that? Farrell wondered. But when the movers had carried in the sofa, they had plopped it against the wall. There it had remained, all this time.

Farrell admired what their thirty minutes of effort had produced. The lone armchair, now angled toward the sofa, created a more inviting area for conversation. The Consignment Depot wrought-iron table was positioned next to the chair; Pat inspected Farrell's crowded bookcase for something interesting to perch on the top. She selected a hand-painted ceramic bowl Farrell had purchased when she had gone out to New Mexico to do a story on life, or rather survival, on a Native American reservation. Farrell watched with respect as Pat grouped together some candles that lay haphazardly on the bookcase shelves and displayed them on the edge of the coffee table.

"Looks better already." Farrell was getting a kick out of the changes.

Pat nodded with satisfaction. "Next time I come, we'll hang and rearrange the stuff on the walls."

"Deal," Farrell answered enthusiastically.

Pat lifted a small brass frame from the bookcase shelf, studying the picture of Farrell and her brother.

"How's Robbie?"

"Better, now that he's not at Nutman Stein anymore. He couldn't take the pressures of the brokerage firm. He's working at KEY now, you know."

"And that's less pressure than Wall Street?" Pat asked skeptically.

"Where Robbie works, it is. He has a job in the film and tape library. He catalogues all the KEY News material shot around the world every day. It's interesting, but not much stress."

"He always was a sensitive kid," Pat mused, staring at the picture. "I remember you watching out for him all the time, making sure that no one picked on him in the schoolyard."

Farrell smiled poignantly. "That's what big sisters do, isn't it?"

Chapter 42

Monday

With more enthusiasm than she remembered having in a long time, Farrell pushed through the heavy revolving door into the KEY News lobby on Monday morning. The weekend out in Westwood had given her just what she needed—some perspective. There was a whole world that functioned and was relatively happy and none of the people in it gave a rat's ass about what happened at KEY News.

She stopped for coffee at the lobby kiosk. "Two, please. Black."

Why not be a sport and bring one for her officemate? It would really throw Dean off to see Farrell smiling and being Lady Bountiful. He'd expect her to be depressed and dragging. Farrell was sure that Dean would know about her termination conversation with Range. Everyone on the *Headlines* staff did by now. Happy news traveled so fast.

She braced herself as she approached her office door.

"You look great for someone who just got the ax."

B. J. was sitting in her chair. Dean was not in the office.

"Whew. That's a relief. It's only you. I thought I was going to have to put on a show. Coffee?"

Farrell offered a paper cup to him. He pried off the plastic lid.

"Ugh. Black."

"Oh yeah, how could I forget? You like it light and sweet."

"Just like my women."

"You're a pig."

"That's what you like about me." B. J. grinned wickedly, white teeth flashing.

She admitted it to herself. She did get a charge out of the irreverent, no-holds-barred banter with B. J. It went directly against all her years of Catholic-school training.

He took a sip of the dark brew and grimaced. "So now what are you going to do?"

"I'm not sure yet. Maybe get out of this nutty business altogether."

"I doubt that. You're hooked."

"I always thought I was, but now I'm not

so sure." She told him about the weekend with Pat at the Consignment Depot. "You know, B. J., there's a big world out there. This isn't the only way to spend your life."

She could tell he wasn't convinced.

"You know, I blame myself somewhat," he said quietly.

Farrell looked at him keenly. "What do you mean?"

"I heard you on the phone with Range the day of the auction. I should have told you to ratchet up the enthusiasm."

"For God's sake, B. J., I'm not a cheer-leader. And this isn't high school. I shouldn't have to pump up Range Bullock, or sweet-talk him into a story. News judgment is news judgment. It's pretty pathetic to think that an executive producer of a national news broadcast is swayed by the presentation."

B. J. shrugged. "Pathetic, maybe. But you should hear the way your buddy Dean pitches a story from out in the field. When he describes it, every story he works on has the potential for a Dupont Award."

Farrell considered B. J.'s words. She knew there was something to them.

"You're right," she murmured. "That Fabergé story was a strong one. I should have fought harder for it."

"So what are you going to do now? Finish out your time here with your tail dragging between your legs?"

Farrell thought of Peter's story of the old lady with the allegedly "real" Moon Egg.

"Actually, I do have something I'm going to work on. An exclusive. Want to work on it with me?"

"Shoot."

Farrell filled him in on everything she knew so far. "I guess the first thing I should do is talk to Clifford Montgomery, the president of Churchill's." She made a note on the yellow legal pad on her desk. She looked up at B. J. "Why are you grinning that ridiculous grin?"

"Guess who I had a date with Saturday night?"

Chapter 43

Monday morning. Pat hummed as she waited for her coffee at Choo-Choo Charlie's.

"Nice weekend?" Charlie Ferrino asked.

"Mmmm. Really nice."

"Do anything special?" By the sound of Pat's "mmmm," Charlie had the feeling he didn't want to hear the answer.

"Yes. I went to dinner in Manhattan. The restaurant was wonderful."

"How 'bout the company? Was it a 'date'?" Charlie busied himself fastening the top to the coffee container, trying to act as if his interest was only a friendly one, when in fact his heart was sinking.

"As a matter of fact, it was." Pat looked like she was trying to suppress her smile.

"And?"

"Oh, Charlie, what do you mean, 'and'? It was just a date, no big deal." Pat laughed nervously, shaking her head.

He didn't believe her.

Chapter 44

Meryl Quan poured tea for Farrell Slater as she waited for Clifford Montgomery to arrive. So this was the woman B. J. was so keen about. Lovely.

"Sugar?"

"No, thank you. But I will have some lemon." Farrell squeezed the juice from the yellow slice into the amber brew.

"I'm sorry that Mr. Montgomery is running a bit behind schedule," Meryl apologized. "But he should be here momentarily."

"No problem." Farrell smiled. She was relieved to have a few minutes to collect herself. She was not looking forward to the conversation they were about to have.

As she waited for Montgomery to come in, Farrell wondered how the president of the auction house was going to react to the news. In her research on him, she had learned about the years he'd studied Fabergé as a young man, while working at La Russie Imperiale—probably one among a half-dozen of the finest antique shops in the world, and the main clearinghouse of the Russian enamels and jewelry in this country. Montgomery was regarded as one of the world's top authorities on Fabergé. Farrell doubted he would be happy when confronted with the possibility that he'd made a mistake in authenticating the Moon Egg.

A six-million-dollar mistake.

"I'm sorry to have kept you waiting."

Montgomery strode across the room and offered his hand to Farrell. He was dressed impeccably in a navy chalk-striped suit. A cornflower-blue pocket handkerchief matched his knotted silk tie.

"Thank you for seeing me so quickly. I'll try not to take up too much of your time."

"Well, we make time for KEY News and your phone call to Ms. Quan here, my assistant, was certainly intriguing."

Outwardly Montgomery seemed calm and

in control. Farrell wondered how he felt inside right now. Probably a bit apprehensive. In a minute he'd be choking.

"Mr. Montgomery, I'm working on a story about *Faux*bergé. You're familiar with that, of course."

Montgomery nodded. "Sure, I've come across a piece here and there myself, from time to time. Usually the sellers who brought them here for auction weren't aware that what they owned were fakes."

"You mean, they purchased the pieces thinking they'd bought authentic Fabergé?"

"That's right."

"How do they take the news when you tell them they've been had?"

Picking up a paperweight, Montgomery paused to consider.

"Disbelief, anger, embarrassment. There's not really much they can do but report the deception to the authorities and hope that the forgers are caught. That rarely happens."

"Why is that?" Farrell asked.

"Forgeries in the art world are much more common than most people realize. Even some of the most learned experts have authenticated fakes."

Farrell wondered if Montgomery already realized she was about to confront him with the possibility that he had authenticated a fake Moon Egg. Was he setting up an excuse for himself, that even the most esteemed in their fields make mistakes? Farrell scribbled in her reporter's notebook.

"Mr. Montgomery," she began. "Do you think there is any possibility that the egg auctioned here at Churchill's last week was not a real Imperial Easter Egg?"

"Anything is possible, Ms. Slater," he said coolly. "However, I authenticated the Moon Egg myself. I stake my reputation and the reputation of this auction house on my decision."

He's a smooth one, thought Farrell.

"Now it's my turn to ask you a question, Ms. Slater. What makes you think that the Moon Egg may be a fake?"

"A source says he knows where the real Moon Egg is."

"A reliable source?"

"I think so, yes."

"Have you seen this alleged Imperial Egg?"

"Not yet."

"Nor will you. It does not exist. These are very serious accusations that you are throwing around here, Ms. Slater. I suggest that you be very careful."

Chapter 45

Olga sat huddled on the side of the worn sofa in her small living room, nervously fingering the pearly buttons on her gray cardigan. Her lined face was troubled as she listened to the earnest pleading of her surrogate grandson.

"Really, Olga. This will be all right. You haven't done anything wrong. You won't be in any trouble."

Olga's cloudy eyes searched Peter's young face. What was it like to be so trusting?

"How are you sure I won't be in trouble?" she asked. "The police are everywhere. Even when you cannot see them." She wrapped her arms tight around her torso, trying to warm herself in the suddenly cold apartment. This American boy was so naïve.

"Olga, I'm not telling you that the police are not everywhere," Peter answered, undaunted. "It's a good bet that they are in places and know things we can't even imagine. I agree with you on that. But what I'm trying to say is that you haven't done anything wrong, and you don't have to worry. No one is going to put you in prison or send you into exile because you have the Moon Egg."

Olga slowly lifted herself from the sofa and slowly made her way to the kitchenette. She switched on the electric burner beneath the tea kettle and opened the fridge, taking out a jar. Peter quickly came to her side.

"Mmm. The caviar! I was hoping you'd have some of this for me!"

Olga smiled as she watched Peter spread the sweet eggplant mixture thickly over slices of white toast. He could never get enough of it. Olga's mother's recipe from the Old Country. She loved watching him enjoy it. "I make more eggplant caviar for next time you come. You can bring to school with you."

As Peter ate, with relish, Olga considered

his arguments. Maybe it was time to come forward, she thought. Time to lift away the heavy burden that she had been carrying for as long as she could remember. What would it be like not to live in fear?

"You say this woman from the television can be trusted?"

Peter nodded solemnly, wiping his mouth on the back of his hand. "I promise, Olga. Farrell is an old friend of Mom's. She grew up here in Westwood. She works for KEY News now and she's sure you won't be in any trouble. She's in a position where she can find out what's going on. Somebody paid six million dollars for a fake. That's not fair."

Olga smiled ruefully. Ah, Peter was so young. He thought the world was fair.

Suddenly Olga was very tired. Tired of hiding, tired of worrying, tired of covering up the truth. She knew it would not be long before she would pass to the next life. She knew it would be best to go with no unfinished business behind her.

She didn't have the energy to live with the secret any longer. Perhaps Peter's coming to her like this was a sign, a sign from God to make things right. While there was still time.

"Okay," she said finally, in her thick accent. Peter looked astonished for a moment. He had actually gotten her to agree! "Okay, Peter, you bring television lady to take pictures of Moon Egg."

Chapter 46

Farrell gazed out the taxi window as it crawled across midtown. It was lunchtime, and traffic was in its usual miserable state.

Where to go from here?

Without the actual egg as evidence, Farrell could not advance the story. From everything Peter had told her about Olga, the old lady was not about to bring her Fabergé egg in for any sort of inspection by Clifford Montgomery, or any authority figure, for that matter. Olga was terrified of the police. But without authentication, it could well be that it was Olga who had a fake egg.

Authority. The FBI.

That was the next logical step.

The yellow cab pulled up in front of the Broadcast Center. She gave the driver a very generous tip. Poor guy, he had to drive around in this mess all day.

He didn't say thank you. Typical. No good deed goes unpunished.

Dean Cohen was getting ready to go out to lunch when Farrell arrived back in their office. "What have you been up to this morning?" he asked.

"Oh, a little of this, a little of that. Since I'm a short-timer. I'm pretty well doing as I please." Farrell tried to sound lighthearted.

"Any job prospects yet?"

"Actually, I have a few things in the fire," she lied.

"Glad to hear it." Dean lied, too.

Farrell tapped the number pads on the telephone to check her voice-mail messages.

"Hey, Farrell, it's me, Rob. If you want to have some lunch, give me a call."

She listened excitedly to the next message, a young man's scratchy voice.

"Farrell, it's Peter Devereaux. Olga will let you take pictures of the Moon Egg. Can you do it today, before she chickens out?"

Chapter 47

God, what have I done?

Clifford Montgomery stared from his red leather chair, a stricken expression on his face.

If Farrell Slater proved right. . . .

His reputation would be ruined. Churchill's would be terribly damaged, perhaps irreparably. And the stock . . . Clifford's mind raced and he could feel his chest tighten.

No, it had to be a mistake, some sort of misunderstanding. Slater could be wrong, couldn't she? After all, she hadn't actually *seen* the egg herself. And the egg sold at auction was flawless, down to the Fabergé marking stamped on its golden base.

He had to see this new egg for himself. But how?

Clifford was so engrossed in his worries, he'd momentarily forgotten that Meryl Quan had been privy to the whole unsettling conversation. Word mustn't get out that there was even a hint of a problem with the auctioned Moon Egg.

He buzzed the intercom, signaling his assistant to come back into his office.

"Meryl, you must promise me, nothing that was said here over the last half-hour must leave this room. Until we figure out what's going on here, we can't talk about this to anyone. Understand?"

 Chapter 48

"Hey, Jack. What's the status of the Fauxbergé investigation you've been working on?"

"Continuing," Special Agent McCord grunted, not looking up from the paperwork on his desk at FBI New York Headquarters in Foley Square.

FBI press information spokesman Fred Behrends wasn't amused. Why was McCord always so damned difficult? Someone should knock that chip off the big guy's shoulders.

"Well, buddy, KEY News is working on a story about fake Fabergé. The producer who called was asking a lot of questions. Lots of what-ifs."

Suddenly McCord seemed interested. "Like what?"

"Like, what if a fake piece of Fabergé was auctioned off for serious money? And what if someone else had the real thing, but was afraid to come forward?"

"What did you tell him?"

"I told *her* that we'd get back to her."

❧ Chapter 49

B. J. adjusted his lights carefully. It wasn't easy to maneuver in Olga's tiny living room. He tried to think of the various shots he'd like to get. The old lady's apartment was a trip. It reminded him of the illustrations in his childhood storybook of the inside of Hansel and Gretel's cottage, where they lived before their parents lost them on purpose in the woods. Or maybe it was the Three

Bears' house. Whatever. Olga's place was visually interesting.

Farrell was busy reassuring the old woman. She was looking pretty shaky. Bet the old gal hadn't had this much excitement in a long time. He hoped she didn't stroke out or something on them now.

"Olga, it would be great if we could shoot some pictures of you sitting in front of the icon," Farrell said softly.

So that's what the little religious painting on the wall was called. An icon. It was draped with a carefully starched and embroidered linen cloth, and a white candle flickered beneath it. A little shrine. B. J. wondered if the old lady knelt and prayed before it. Probably, if she could bend those birdy legs and get down there on those bony knees. He felt momentarily guilty. He couldn't remember the last time he'd gotten down on his knees to pray.

"Peter tell me you want picture of egg. Not picture of me," Olga protested to Farrell.

God, he hoped Farrell could talk the old lady into letting him tape her. She was straight out of central casting and she'd be a really great element for the piece they would eventually do. *C'mon, Farrell. Talk the old girl into it.*

"Of course, Olga. You don't have to do anything you don't want to do. If you don't want us to take pictures of you, we won't. But I have to be honest with you, it will make the story much stronger if our viewers are able to see the woman who has the real Moon Egg."

Olga considered the producer's request. She looked uncertain.

"How about this?" Farrell continued. "While we're here, we'll take the pictures of you. I'll call you when we get ready to air the story and you can tell me then if we can use them or not. I promise I won't include you in the story without your permission."

Olga looked confused. B. J. didn't like feeling they were taking advantage of her. But he felt that way lots of times on different stories. He felt sorry, if he let himself, for the poor schnooks who found themselves with unwanted notoriety and had to live with the aftermath of their particular circumstances long after he and his camera left.

"Come on, Olga," Farrell encouraged. "Why don't you sit over here? We'll put this little chair over by the icon. There. Sit here, Olga."

Olga obediently took a seat in the wooden chair. She smoothed out her skirt and then folded her hands in her lap. She looked nervously from the camera to Farrell.

"Tell us a little about yourself, Olga."

"What do you want to know?"

"Where were you born?"

"St. Petersburg."

"Russia?"

"Yes."

"When did you come to this country?"

"When I escape from Russia after Papa die."

"When was that?"

"After World War."

"One?" asked Farrell.

"No, Two."

"How did you get out of Russia?"

Olga was beginning to look frightened. B. J. hoped Farrell would pick up on that and lay off this line of questioning.

"You don't have to talk about that, if you don't want to, Olga," Farrell said gently. "But tell us how you came to have the Moon Egg."

Olga took a deep breath and B. J. zoomed

in tighter on her face. The camera was picking up a nervous twitch at the corner of Olga's right eye.

"My father work in Fabergé studio in St. Petersburg. He is famous workmaster. Makes many beautiful things for czar and royal court. The most special thing, he make Easter eggs for czar to give czarina and his mother on our most special holy day. My father work on these eggs."

Olga stopped and her eyes darted from Farrell to the camera and back again, reminding B. J. of a scared rabbit.

"Just look at me, Olga," Farrell instructed gently. "Don't think about the camera. Just relax and talk to me like I'm the only one here."

"When czar and royal family overthrown, there is chaos everywhere in our country. Revolutionaries take over everything. They come to studio and take everything for the new people's government."

"Everything?"

Was the camera picking up a smile in Olga's eyes?

"Well, not everything. Some of the workers hide things. My father, he hide Moon Egg."

"Could you show us the Moon Egg now, Olga?"

Chapter 50

B. J. popped the videotape into the machine, cuing it up ten seconds before the part when the Moon Egg opened and the comet of diamond stars appeared. Then he and Farrell sat back to wait for Range Bullock.

Farrell wondered if B. J. could feel her tension. The moment she'd seen Olga's Moon Egg, she'd known it was the real thing. She was sure of it. It didn't matter that she was no expert in gemology or antiquities, didn't know all that much about Russian history or jewelry design. The power of the work of art overwhelmed her and she knew to her bones that she was looking at Nicholas's gift for his beloved Alexandra.

Would Range be able to see it as well? Or would he dismiss it because she was the messenger bringing it to him?

"Let's see it." The executive producer loomed in the viewing-room doorway.

As B. J. hit the play button, Farrell watched Range's face, trying to read his reaction. Skepticism.

That's his job, Farrell thought to herself. *He has to make sure of the facts. Don't take it personally, he isn't judging you. He's judging the facts of the story.*

"Interesting," he grunted, when B. J. stopped the tape. "So you say it's an old Russian emigré that has this alleged Fabergé egg?"

"Yes. And she's hidden it all these years, afraid to let anyone know that she has it." Farrell waited.

"And the head of one the world's foremost auction houses, and an acknowledged expert on Fabergé, authenticated the egg that was sold last week?"

"I know it seems unbelievable, but yes." Farrell's heart thumped in her chest.

There was thick silence in the room as Range leaned on the doorjamb, mulling over the improbable story. Farrell could feel her pulse pounding in her ears and her face flushed as she waited for his response.

"I suppose anything is possible," he answered finally. "But we need more than this before we can go with the story."

"I have an interview at the FBI this afternoon. I'll see what I can get there," Farrell said, hiding her disappointment.

"Good. Let me know what you find out." As Range left the viewing room, he wondered if he had misjudged Farrell.

Chapter 51

As Farrell waited for her interview at New York FBI headquarters, she already suspected a few things about her subject. He would be in good physical condition, he would be an expert marksman, and he would probably be a somewhat cynical patriot, with a good measure of control freak sprinkled in for good measure. Acquiring wealth would not be of major importance to this guy. Nobody got rich working for the Federal Bureau of Investigation.

Farrell did not bargain for the fact that she would be instantly attracted to Special Agent Jack McCord.

His eyes. Piercing blue, they locked onto hers the moment he entered the room. He was accompanied by the FBI press information officer, Fred Behrends. Farrell knew that Behrends was there to run interference for McCord, make sure that the investigator did not run off at the mouth too much.

After they all shook hands and took their seats in the metal chairs that graced the spare government office, Behrends asked, "How can we help you, Miss Slater?"

Why did she feel suddenly nervous? She had gone on hundreds of interviews in her career. Usually she could tell the interviewees were far more intimidated than she was. Why did Jack McCord's eyes boring into her make her heart beat faster? She could feel her cheeks grow hot. The foot at the bottom of her crossed leg wiggled and she wished she had worn a better outfit than her gray flannel trousers and navy merino wool turtleneck. Why hadn't she taken a few minutes to freshen up her makeup before she came?

No wonder she hadn't had a date in over a year.

Farrell cleared her throat. "I'm working on a story about art forgery—Fabergé forgery, to be exact. And I want to find out what you can tell me about what the FBI is doing about it."

"Can you be more specific?" Agent Behrends asked.

"Well, it's come to our attention that a recently auctioned Fabergé Imperial Easter Egg may be a fake."

Neither agent's facial expression changed. *Nice job,* thought Farrell.

"Are you talking about the Moon Egg just auctioned at Churchill's?" asked McCord.

"As a matter of fact, yes."

"And what makes you think that it wasn't the real thing?"

"Information that I have from a source who is sure of the real Moon Egg's location."

"Have you seen the alleged real egg?"

Hey, I'm supposed to be asking the questions here, thought Farrell. She did not like feeling grilled by McCord.

"Yes, I have," admitted Farrell.

"Well, Ms. Slater, the FBI would be very interested in seeing this other egg. How do you think we can make that happen?"

"Not through me, you can't, Agent Mc-Cord."

"Of course, you realize that, as a United States citizen, you have a responsibility to not withhold information that could lead to the solving of a crime."

"Certainly I do, but my information isn't about a crime," Farrell answered primly. "If what I've been told is true, the real Moon Egg is out there, but that is not a criminal offense. The law that's been broken is that a fake egg was auctioned off as the real thing. That's where you guys come in. What, if anything, is the FBI doing to investigate?"

Farrell could tell she had hit a nerve with McCord, as she noticed his jaw clench. Behrends jumped in before the other agent could say anything in anger.

"We don't comment on ongoing investigations, Miss Slater. But you can be sure, the Bureau is using its considerable resources to track down anyone or any group who is breaking the law."

Chapter 52

"Legal called. The FBI wants a list of our recurring Fabergé sellers and buyers." Meryl ticked off the next item on her list.

Churchill's legal department had a good working relationship with the FBI—all major auction houses did. Both sides routinely swapped bits of information.

But it was the specific type of clients the Bureau wanted to know about that raised the red flag to Montgomery.

He thought quickly. If he didn't turn the list over voluntarily, it would look bad, arousing suspicion that something was wrong. And if he refused, the FBI could just go ahead and subpoena the information anyway.

It was smarter just to hand it over. The name of the egg consignor wasn't on the list anyway. "Okay, fine. Give it to them. We want to cooperate with them whenever possible." Montgomery's voice didn't betray how worried he was.

What the hell was the FBI going to do with that list?

Chapter 53

It was never easy. Never simple. That was just the way of the world. You took care of one problem, and there was always another to take its place.

Misha was out of the way. Now this.

It would be simple to get to her. A defenseless, frail, ancient woman, living alone in a tiny garden apartment. No big deal.

Don't be too cocky, big shot. This *was* a big deal. A very big deal. A six-million-dollars-or-go-to-prison deal. And that wasn't the way this was going to end up. Be sure of it. Not after all the years of hard work that it took to get to this point. Not after all the exacting study and planning.

Maybe Olga wouldn't have to die. After the

Misha mess, the thought of another murder was distasteful. Perhaps it could be avoided.

Yes. Actually, it was necessary only to obtain the real egg. That would be enough. No need for killing. Without the egg, she'd be no threat. The timid old soul wasn't about to go to the police.

But if it did end up that she had to be killed, it sure as hell wasn't going to be like the last time. Getting Misha out of the way had been gross, and too much work, to boot. If it came to it, this time it would be much easier. At least for the one doing the killing.

Chapter 54

Cossack-costumed Tony held the door open for Meryl as she hurried from Churchill's. She was late for her date with B. J.

"How long are they going to make you wear that getup, Tony?" Meryl asked him. As he hailed her a cab, he waited with her at the curb.

"A few more weeks, Miss Quan. But I don't mind. It's good for business and, hey, it keeps me warm, too."

Meryl slid into the open taxi and listened to Eartha Kitt growl at her to make sure to buckle up her seat belt. The smell of curry permeated the air inside the cab and, despite the chill, she cracked the window to let in some of the fresh, evening breeze.

The car cut through Central Park to the Upper West Side, dropping her at the Lincoln Plaza Cinemas. B. J. was waiting just inside the theater door. He kissed her hello.

"Come on. I've got the tickets already. We're going to be late."

They climbed the steps of the escalator, not waiting for the automated stairs to take them to the second-floor theaters.

"Popcorn?" B. J. offered as they passed the neon refreshment stand.

"No thanks. I'll wait."

They found two seats together in the already darkened theater and settled in just as the previews were finishing. The opening credits rolled. Starring Tom Cruise, her favorite.

But Meryl found, try as she might, she couldn't concentrate on what was happen-

ing on the big screen. The Fabergé thing
was bothering her. First the KEY News producer, then the FBI. Something was wrong,
she knew it. And she didn't want to be
caught up in it. If something illegal was going on, Meryl didn't want to be associated
with it. She'd spent her life so far achieving,
always living aboveboard and trying to im-
prove herself. Her young career was going
well. She didn't want to be part of any scandal.

"What did you think?" B. J. asked as the
lights came up.

"Good."

"You're kidding, right? It sucked."

Meryl wriggled into her coat. "I don't know,
B. J. I just couldn't concentrate."

"C'mon. Let's go get some dinner and we
can talk."

They walked a few blocks uptown in the
frigid February air, and ducked into a small
Italian restaurant in the bottom of a brown-
stone just off Central Park. Some faux fres-
coes, all in pastels, were painted on the
dining-room walls. Votive candles flickered
on the white-tableclothed tables.

The ponytailed maître d' led them to a
small table near the back.

"La signorina è bellissima stassera." As he pulled out her chair, he complimented Meryl in what she suspected was a phony Italian accent. Probably none of the people who worked here was Italian. The waiters were likely out-of-work actors.

Lately Meryl felt that she lived in a world where things were not as they seemed. She didn't know what to be sure of anymore. Was Clifford a crook? Had he knowingly authenticated a fake Fabergé egg?

B. J. ordered a bottle of chianti. Meryl downed the first glass quickly and set right to drinking another glass of the red wine.

"Hey, slow down," laughed B. J. "If you don't watch out, you'll get plastered and I'll definitely take advantage of you."

Meryl smiled weakly and pulled a piece of Italian bread from the loaf in the basket in the middle of the table. She wanted to talk to B. J. about what was going on, but she was afraid. She didn't want to be disloyal to Clifford in disclosing what was happening in the office. On the other hand, if Clifford had done nothing wrong, there really was no harm in telling B. J.

"You know, I've been meaning to ask you. . . ." She tried to sound offhanded. "Do you know someone at KEY named Farrell Slater?"

"Sure I do. Farrell and I work together all the time. She was the producer I was shooting for the day you and I met at the auction, as a matter of fact. Why do you ask?"

"Well, she was in to see my boss recently, and when she left, he was pretty upset."

"Upset about the Fabergé Moon Egg?" he offered.

Meryl's mouth dropped. "How did you know?"

"After what I saw today, your boss better be upset."

Chapter 55

Now that the television people were gone, the closet didn't feel safe anymore. Her treasure needed to be somewhere else, somewhere safer, somewhere nobody would ever find it.

Olga knew where she would hide it. No one would think to look there.

She lifted the jeweled egg from its golden nesting box. Her withered hands trembling, Olga carefully wrapped the Moon Egg in three CVS plastic bags, the kind that Americans used once and tossed away, but Olga saved.

Round and round she swaddled the egg until she was satisfied that no dampness could permeate the plastic. Then, her arthritic knees throbbing, Olga shuffled across her small apartment and thrust the small package into the cool, dark ooze.

Chapter 56

Friday of the First Week of Lent

Russian Peasant Folk Belief

*"Whoever fasts on this Friday
will not die a sudden death."*

A knock on the door always unsettled Olga.

She thought back to her childhood. When the knock came, she was afraid that the vicious Russian police were coming to drag away her father as they had stolen the fathers of her friends. Leningrad—as St. Petersburg became after the czar was overthrown and the Communists took control—was a treacherous place, a deadly place, full of whispers and the sounds of heavy footsteps in the night. Young Olga knew the terror of the banging on apartment doors, the loud, deep voices that demanded entry. The wailing and weeping that followed the screams.

But her friends had two parents. They had mothers who stayed behind to take care of the young ones when the fathers went to meet their fate. Surely the new government would not take her father.

Her mother was dead, killed by the cruel conditions of their new life. The bitter Russian winter, not enough to eat, and no medicine had seen to that. To Olga, the Communists had already killed her mother. They would not take her father, too.

But eventually the insistent knock in the night came.

Decades had passed, but she still heard the pounding on the wooden door. At night she dreamed of it—fitful, tossing dreams that left her heart pounding and her skin cold and clammy. By day, she dreaded even the lightest tapping on the doors of the other apartments on her hall. And when there was a knock on her own door, she trembled.

But, thankfully, knocks on her door were rare. Pat, Peter, once in a while the landlord. Charlie occasionally dropping off something from the deli. She kept to herself. She didn't want any trouble.

The candle flickered beneath the icon of the Blessed Virgin and her infant Son. *Holy Mother, protect us,* she prayed as she crept to answer the third knock.

"Who is there?"

Chapter 57

Olga's visitor painstakingly searched and examined every nook and cranny of the small apartment, taking extreme care to put things back as they were. It must appear that nothing was amiss.

For a moment, the promise of a satisfying search. The distinctive yellow velvet Fabergé case discovered beneath the blankets at the bottom of the bedroom closet. But as it was lifted, it was too light.

Empty!

Where was the Moon Egg?

Think. Don't panic. Never panic.

The visitor looked some more. The seconds ticked away to minutes. The search turned up nothing. Nothing. Where was it?

It was time to get out. It was too dangerous to stay any longer.

If the Moon Egg couldn't be gotten, at least its owner—the person who could produce it, could attest to its existence—had to be put out of the way. That made sense.

The visitor carefully positioned the old lady on the single bed. It would look like she was asleep when the fire started.

The holy candle was lifted to ignite the white linen stole that draped the gilt icon of Christ and his Mother.

Chapter 58

The shrill ring of the phone cut through Farrell's exhausted sleep. The bedside clock read two A.M.

In the instant it took her to reach for the receiver, apprehension coursed through her body. Most people thought a call in the middle of the night signaled a family emergency, but for someone in the news business, the nocturnal ring could mean anything. A plane crash, a war, an assassination.

"Farrell . . . it's Peter. Peter Devereaux."

Farrell could hear fear in the young man's voice.

"Peter, what is it? What's wrong?"

"It's Olga. A fire. Oh my God."

Farrell struggled into a sitting position and snapped on the bedside lamp, her eyes burning as they adjusted to the sudden light.

"Peter, just take a deep breath and tell me what's happened. First of all, where are you?"

"I'm at Pascack Valley Hospital."

"Where's your mother?"

"She's talking to the doctor in intensive care."

So it was bad.

"What happened?"

"There was a fire in Olga's apartment. I don't know how it started. But she. . . ." His voice trailed off and Farrell could hear he was struggling not to cry. Poor kid.

"How badly is she burned?" Visions of raw flesh, oozing blisters, and painful skin grafts flashed through her head. Burns were the worst. The pain was beyond excruciating. Farrell's bedroom was warm, but she shivered with the thought.

"I don't know. But she's unconscious and

the doctor told Mom that it doesn't look good."

At that, Peter couldn't hold it in anymore. Farrell heard his breaking voice.

"Farrell, it's my fault. I know it is. I should have kept my promise."

⚘ Chapter 59

The car service dropped Farrell at Pascack Valley Hospital. Pat and Peter were waiting in the lobby.

"Thanks for coming all the way out here," Pat said as she enveloped Farrell in a hug. "Peter told me he called you. It makes us both feel better having you here."

"It's no big deal. How's Olga? How bad are the burns?"

"Thank God, she isn't burned. It's the smoke that was the problem. She must have fallen as she passed out, and hit her head. She's not waking up."

"What are the doctors saying?"

"It doesn't look good. Someone Olga's age

doesn't just bounce back." Pat's voice shook.

Peter reached out and put his arms around his mother. She rested her head against her son's shoulder. "Oh Peter, this is so sad." Pat began to weep.

Farrell saw the anguished expression on Peter's face.

"This isn't your fault, you know," Farrell whispered.

Pat looked puzzled. "*Your* fault? How could you ever think this was *your* fault? It was an accident."

Peter nodded silently. Farrell watched the young man and wished he would tell his mother what was bothering him. Get it out. He'd feel so much better. Instead, he hung his head and said nothing.

Pat scrutinized her son's face. "Peter, sweetheart, of course it wasn't your fault. The fire chief said that the candle that Olga always kept burning started the fire. You had nothing to do with that."

Chapter 60

Professor Tim Kavanagh drove up the Garden State Parkway, compelled to get to Pat and Peter. He hoped Pat wouldn't think he was too presumptuous. After all, they'd only had one date.

But when Pat called to say she wouldn't be able to make their second dinner together, he could hear the worry in her voice. And knowing Peter's relationship with the old lady, Kavanagh knew they both could use some moral support.

He wanted to be close by.

He thought of the pile of ungraded quizzes that sat atop the desk in his study and sighed heavily. They'd have to wait.

This was his life. One semester followed another. Each new Russian Studies class barely met the minimum enrollment requirement. With the Cold War over, very few students seemed interested in Russia, past or present. Only occasionally did you get a kid who really loved the subject. A kid like Peter.

Of course, Seton Hall's School of Diplomacy looked very promising. He'd been involved in getting the new school off the ground when the United Nations Association went looking for an academic partner to educate future specialists in international relations. The professor readily agreed to be a faculty fellow, offering courses specifically designed for the increasing number of students who were coming to Seton Hall from around the world and who were now giving the university a more global reputation.

Tim tossed a token into the Hillsdale Plaza toll basket and rolled up the car window against the cold night air. A champagne-colored Lexus LS400 pulled out in front of his maroon Altima, beating him to exit 168. He'd love to buy a Lexus, he thought, yearning, but a tenured professor with a salary of $60,000 a year couldn't very well be driving around in a $50,000 car. It wouldn't make sense. People would talk.

No. He'd have to content himself with his growing Fabergé collection. Knowing that he and the Russian royal family had that in common gave Tim Kavanagh much pleasure and satisfaction. If it was good enough for the czars, it was good enough for him.

Chapter 61

There wasn't much worth saving in Olga's apartment. What the fire hadn't charred, the smoke had blackened and the firemen's hoses had soaked.

Farrell and Tim accompanied Pat and Peter to survey the wreckage.

"It's a miracle she survived this at all." Farrell whispered what was on the others' minds.

Farrell and Peter went straight in the direction of the bedroom. The wooden bedframe looked like the charcoal remains in the bottom of a barbecue pit. A small mirror had managed to stay anchored to the wall, but thick, black soot kept it from reflecting anything.

The bedroom closet was shut tight. Farrell

and Peter looked at each other before prying it open. Olga's clothes were carefully and precisely hanging from the rod, some hats and Olga's brown leather pocketbook were lined up on the overhead shelf. Peter bent to rummage under the blanket on the closet floor. He found what he was looking for. He quickly opened the yellow velvet carrying case.

It was empty.

"It's gone!" he whispered to Farrell.

The four continued to pick their way through the scorched debris on the floor, looking for recognizable remnants of Olga's life. The air was thick with the acrid stench of the burned wool rug, now soggy beneath their feet. They didn't say much as they went about their grim reconnaissance. Only an occasional cough broke the silence as their lungs rejected the apartment's toxic air.

Peter opened the refrigerator door. A stick of gleaming, yellow butter on a clear, glass dish. A piece of salmon peeked through Saran Wrap, ready for Olga to prepare for her solitary dinner. Half a loaf of dark, pumpernickel bread waited to be spread with the homemade eggplant caviar that filled three thick Mason jars.

Peter stood staring into the refrigerator.

"Come on, sweetheart," Pat said as she put her arm around her son's shoulder. "There's nothing more we can do here. Let's go." Then she added in true motherly fashion. "Here, honey. Take Olga's caviar with you. She always loved to make it for you and she'd want you to have it."

Looking over at Farrell and Tim, she offered, "You take some, too."

 Chapter 62

Second Sunday of Lent

Jack came in drenched from the cold rain and his double jog around the Central Park reservoir. He loved his Sunday-morning run. It gave him an opportunity to get rid of some tension and organize his thoughts. His thoughts lately were primarily about his Fauxbergé case.

Meryl Quan was an invaluable source of information. She'd provided Jack with a list

of all Churchill's recurring Fabergé customers and sellers. She said that her boss had
okayed it. Of course, if McCord was going
to use it down the line in court, he'd have to
get a subpoena.

If it came to that, a court order wouldn't be
a problem. Churchill's and the FBI had a
good working relationship. It was mutually
beneficial. When Churchill department experts suspected stolen property had been
consigned for auction, they advised the FBI
right away. The Bureau, in turn, called the
auction house about property known to have
been purloined.

On the one hand, Churchill's had a private
relationship with its clients, but on the other
hand, it didn't want hassles, didn't want to
be receiving and selling illegal merchandise.
And, usually, Churchill clients consigning
objects for sale didn't even know that they
had unwittingly purchased stolen goods.

It constantly amazed Jack how eager the
public usually was to cooperate with the FBI.
Sure, the Bureau had taken some serious
hits since the days when J. Edgar Hoover
had reigned over the agency. Back then, the
American people had viewed the Federal
Bureau of Investigation with awe and abso-

lute respect. But when Hoover died, and some of the not-so-pleasant realities of how the Bureau conducted its business came to light, the FBI's sterling reputation had gotten a little tarnished. The bungling at Waco and Ruby Ridge had added to the public awareness that the nation's justice force was comprised not of the infallible special agents of the Hoover myth, but mostly of dedicated and well-trained men and women who sometimes made mistakes.

Still, it seemed to Jack that on the whole, the public was eager to believe in the FBI. The average American citizen took comfort in the idea the federal government was doing its best to protect them. And they wanted to help when they could.

Then Jack's more cynical nature kicked in. *Let's face it,* he thought, *no one wants to piss off the FBI.* They were just too scared.

They should be.

Jack thought of Farrell Slater. She wasn't cooperating any. The KEY producer with the big brown eyes didn't seem to care one way or the other if she angered the FBI. From her position with a network news organization, she probably felt secure that the FBI wasn't going to give her a hard time.

Don't be too sure, Farrell.

Chapter 63

It was so easy to get past hospital security. All you had to do was tell them you were a relative and they let you through. *Just act as if it's the most natural thing in the world that you are coming to visit. Tell them Olga's doctor said it was okay.*

Once you got past the front desk, you were home free. The nurses and orderlies, overworked and understaffed, were too busy to question why you were there.

Olga lay frail and thin against the stark white hospital sheet. The blue cotton blanket was tucked neatly around her where it would most likely remain undisturbed until the morning when a nurse would come in to pull it back to tend to the old woman, perhaps giving her a sponge bath, maybe massaging her aged limbs.

Gray-tissued lids hooded Olga's deep-set eyes. Would they ever open?

Chances were that nature would take its course. Olga had lived a long life. It would have ended soon anyway. This was only going to speed things up a little.

But if she did come out of it, if she did pull through . . . It was essential to know when it was time to finish the job.

Chapter 64

Another Monday morning at KEY News. There weren't that many Mondays left.

Farrell would rather not see anyone in the halls of the Broadcast Center. When she bumped into someone she knew in the cafeteria or the ladies' room, she could tell they were uncomfortable. They didn't know what to say. Farrell was being kicked out of what was, to them, the be-all and end-all. KEY News.

Farrell understood. It was seductive stuff, the television news business. It gave you cachet when it came time to swap occupations when introductions were being made at cocktail or dinner parties.

But how many dinner parties did she actually go to, anyway?

It was more the feeling of being on the inside, knowing what was going on before the public heard it reported, that had always given Farrell a charge. She had that feeling now. The excitement of knowing she was on to something. The urgency of getting her facts straight so she could go with the story, beat the competition.

She was fairly certain she had an exclusive going on this Moon Egg story. She was eager to broadcast it. But she grudgingly admitted to herself that Range was right. She needed more to go on than some videotape of Olga holding her egg. The other part of the story had to be figured out. Had the president of Churchill's authenticated the egg knowing it was a forgery? Or had he simply made a mistake that would cost him his professional reputation and ruin the standing of the esteemed auction house? Where had the bogus egg come from? And who had bought it, unwittingly paying six million dollars for a fake?

Then there was the scariest, saddest part. Olga. Farrell prayed it was just a coincidence the fire had broken out at the Russian woman's apartment when it had. She hoped it was only a fluke, that it had nothing to do with Olga's coming forward with her precious Moon Egg.

Farrell tried to reassure herself. The video of Olga holding the Imperial Egg hadn't been aired on *Evening Headlines*. The public hadn't seen it yet. So the video could not have led anyone to Olga.

The fire had to be an accident. Please, God, it had to be.

 Chapter 65

Clifford Montgomery paced the Persian carpet in his Churchill's office. Haggard and worried, he hadn't slept well since Farrell Slater's visit. What was she up to? What was she finding out? He had to know. It didn't help matters that he was absolutely inundated by things that had to be attended to, what with the various Russian auctions coming up. He had taken to falling asleep several nights a week on his office couch, freshening up in the mornings in his small dressing room—one of the perks of being the president of Churchill's. He had a place to leave some clean shirts and a Brooks Brothers suit, and a place to take a shower, right next to his office.

Was he going to switch on *KEY Evening Headlines* some night soon and listen while anchorwoman Eliza Blake announced the biggest scandal to hit the art world in years? Was everything he had worked so hard to achieve going to come tumbling down for all the world to watch on their television screens? Would the audience be fascinated by his ruin?

Better to have the enemy inside the tent, so you could see what she was doing.

Montgomery buzzed the intercom.

"Meryl, would you please call Farrell Slater over at KEY News and ask her if she'd like to be my guest at the lecture I'm giving on art forgery at the Metropolitan?"

"Farrell Slater?" Meryl asked, surprise in her voice.

"That's what I said," he snapped.

If he could befriend Farrell, perhaps he could convince her that the auctioned Moon Egg was legitimate. After all, she'd said she hadn't seen the other egg herself, practically admitting she hadn't any proof.

It was worth a try. If he couldn't persuade her, he'd have to deal with Farrell in another way.

Chapter 66

Dialing the phone number of the Consignment Depot, Farrell glared at Dean Cohen's back as he sat at the desk in front of hers. How she hated sharing an office with him. *Not for long*, she thought. That would be one good thing about leaving KEY News.

Pat picked up on the second ring. "Consignment Depot."

"Pat, it's me, Farrell. How's Olga?"

"Holding on, so far," Pat answered quietly.

"Still unconscious?"

"Uh-huh."

"What are the doctors saying?"

"Not much. Those guys play it so close to the vest. They say we'll have to wait and see."

Farrell heard a bell ring in the background.

"Got to go, Farrell. A customer is here. I'll keep you posted if there is anything new on Olga's condition."

Next, Farrell dialed area code 201 information.

"Westwood, please. I'd like the number for the fire department."

She had the feeling that Dean was listening to her side of the telephone calls. Busybody.

"Hello, this is Farrell Slater with KEY News in New York. I'd like to speak with the fire chief, please."

Farrell doodled on the blotter on her desk as she waited for the chief to come to the phone. *Olga. Egg. Video. Fire*. She traced six question marks after the last word.

The chief came to the phone as quickly as he could. "KEY News" had brought him running in from outside.

"No, Ms. Slater, we don't think there was any foul play here. We're pretty sure the old lady's candle started the fire. It was an accident."

"You're sure of it?"

"Almost a hundred percent sure."

" 'Almost'?"

The chief hesitated for a moment. "Well, the only thing that's bothering us, is that the apartment door was unlocked when we got there. Most of the old people around here keep their doors locked. Even though we like to think ours is a safe little town, we've done a local public-awareness campaign on the importance of home security. And the old lady's landlord told us she was fanatical about making sure her door was locked."

 Chapter 67

Tuesday

Victor had found it years ago, when he was just a little kid, though his mother did not know it.

He checked the hidden drawer in the walnut secretary every so often to see if there was anything new inside. Over the years, the drawer had yielded lots of interesting things, bits of information that helped him to figure out his mother, Nadine. The prima ballerina. The legend.

The love letters had always been his favorite secret. The letters to "Nadjia"—a nickname, he assumed, for his mother. Nadjia, Nadine. Close enough.

But who was "V."? Who was the man who signed the heartsick love notes? It wasn't his dead father. His name had been Michael. His mother must have had a clandestine affair with someone. Someone who meant a great deal to her, or she wouldn't have saved the letters, incriminating as they were.

It had always intrigued Victor to think of his mother sneaking around, involved with a man other than his father. She must have met him during her stint as a diplomat's wife in Russia. The letters revealed how lonely her lover was without her in St. Petersburg. Had she been lonely as her husband worked long hours in the American embassy during the Cold War? Was that what drove her to taking a chance like that?

The "V." bothered him, though. Not many names began with that letter. The fact that

Mother had named her only son Victor, made him wonder. He'd never asked her about it, though. That would signal to her that he knew about her hiding place.

Victor hadn't checked the drawer in a while. There hadn't been anything new in there for a long time. Not too much happened in his mother's quiet, insulated life anymore. But he was bored today, and it was worth a shot. Nadine was upstairs having a massage that would keep her occupied for at least the next hour.

His thick frame looked out of place in the finely detailed office. Peasant stock. That's what he'd heard a maid whisper about him years ago. He tried to make the most of the attributes he did possess. Physical strength was his long suit and he worked hard to maximize his power. Lifting weights and working out were part of his daily routine. The gym was his passion.

The gym and—lately—Stacey Spinner. She made him feel so good. She complimented him all the time on his physique. Told him how handsome he was. No one, except his mother, had ever done that. And somehow his mother didn't count. Mothers had to praise their sons.

Being with Stacey made Victor feel good in a whole variety of ways, and he wanted to make sure she stayed in his life.

Victor took a seat at the walnut desk, his thick muscles straining against the seams of his trousers. Opening the paneled doors at the top, he felt beneath the shelf for the button. Open sesame.

 Chapter 68

Farrell watched Walter Cronkat and his pal Jane Pawley nibble indifferently at their dinners while she dwelled nervously on her conversation with the Westwood fire chief. The fact that Olga's door had been unlocked bothered her. Though she prayed otherwise, Farrell felt increasingly certain that the fire had been no accident. And most unsettling was the idea that Olga lay near death in Pascack Valley Hospital merely because she possessed the Moon Egg. The Moon Egg that Farrell had insisted she reveal.

The television producer paced her apartment, straightening the crooked bulletin board and plumping the kilim pillows she had purchased in Pat's shop, another tiny attempt to spruce up the tired sofa. She thought of Peter, earnest and so young, telling her Olga's story, trusting Farrell to know what to do. She had let the kid down, letting her own hunger for a good story, a redeeming story for herself, get in the way of being responsible. Hell, she had reassured Peter that Olga wouldn't be in any trouble without knowing for sure what the legal repercussions would be for the old woman with the smuggled egg. And now the fire.

She pulled her thick white velour robe tighter around her and made up her mind.

She didn't really want to do it, but she had to. She had to call Jack McCord at the FBI and tell him about her fears. Before someone else got hurt.

Chapter 69

Farrell stood at the base of the grand steps of the Metropolitan Museum of Art on Fifth Avenue. A bright blue sky framed the massive granite structure, with dun-colored Central Park on both sides. Long, luminously colored banners flapped noisily in the late-winter wind, announcing the special exhibits on display inside. One, in vivid purple, proclaimed, Russia's Royal Romanovs. Farrell made a mental note to take a peek at the exhibit after Clifford Montgomery's lecture.

New York was such a magical place sometimes, she thought. So alive, so intense. Could she ever really go back to a small-town kind of life?

She climbed the stairs with a bounce in her step, eager to get inside.

The main foyer bustled with museum patrons, checking their coats, conferring with the volunteers at the information desk, studying their programs and deciding what beauties to behold first. There was a palpable energy in the air, the excitement of being able to get close enough to touch some of the most fabulous and famous art in the world.

A gray-haired man at the round information desk directed Farrell to the lecture auditorium. She checked her trench coat and walked through a long hallway full of Greek and Roman statues, past a small gift stand, and down some stairs to the lecture hall. The room was almost full and Clifford Montgomery was already speaking.

"Art forgery has gone on throughout the five thousand years of mankind's creative history. Not a month goes by in the art world without another tale of some new, fabulous fake being unmasked, or someone being royally ripped off by acquiring an expensive, well-executed imitation, but an imitation nonetheless."

Montgomery continued, smoothly and interestingly. Using slides, he showed the audience examples of famous forgeries through the ages. Portions of the Bible were faked. In the fourteenth century, a known forger confessed to having faked the Shroud of Turin, yet it wasn't until the 1990s that this fraud was laid to rest. Renoir was known to have copied some of his better work, selling them as "original" when he needed to keep food on the table. The list went on and on.

"And so, ladies and gentlemen," Montgomery concluded, "I leave you with the words of Horace who had the whole thing nailed down so long ago when he said, 'He who knows a thousand works of art, knows a thousand frauds.'"

The audience applauded enthusiastically and Montgomery reveled in the praise.

"Are there any questions?" he called to the audience.

"Can you comment on the rise of Fabergé forgery?"

Farrell, standing at the back of the auditorium, knew Montgomery didn't like her question, but she had to admire the showman in him. He took a drink of water and smiled amiably.

"Of course. That's a very good question, especially in light of the increased interest in Fabergé caused by the recent auction of the legendary Moon Egg for six million dollars at Churchill's, and the Fabergé featured in the popular Romanov exhibit that's going on here at the Metropolitan. Fabergé has been copied and imitated for years, the forgers using the photographs in art books as models for their purpose. But serious collectors could usually spot the fakes. The work just wasn't as fine and, since Fabergé's works were usually one of a kind, duplicates must be forgeries.

"Now, with the recent record prices being paid for Fabergé, and the discovery of the actual Fabergé design book, forgers have come out of the woodwork. Current fakes, made in St. Petersburg and New York, are quite ambitious and exceedingly well executed. Many unsuspecting buyers, even some museum curators, have been duped. Forging Fabergé has become a major source of income for criminals."

Was Montgomery taunting her? Farrell wondered. Or, by inviting her to hear his lecture, was he trying to reassure her that he had nothing to hide?

Chapter 70

With no appointments pending all afternoon at Spun Gold Interiors, Stacey clicked the television remote control in the office, eager to watch Joan Rivers on QVC. She wished Rivers' show was on more often. She loved Joan's jewelry.

Of course, it was only costume, but the designs were clever and the workmanship was quite good. Stacey had ordered things from the show, though she really didn't like to admit to anyone that she even watched QVC.

She especially liked the pieces based on Fabergé designs. Joan was a Fabergé aficionado. Her husband Edgar had given her a Fabergé necklace years before, which had once belonged to Empress Marie of Romania. Joan's jewelers had copied it so that Jane Q. Public could have her own version of the tiny, enameled-egg charms in various shades and designs that hung from a gold-plated chain.

Stacey had always wished she could afford the real thing. She resented being a pretender. She was meant to have precious jewelry, not costume. When she'd taken Churchill's fine-jewelry course, she had fantasized about owning and wearing the glittering gems set in gold and platinum.

Like Nadine Paradise's crescent brooch. How royal she'd feel wearing that beautiful pin! But she consoled herself with the thought that if she played her cards right, if she could keep things going with Victor, she would have plenty of her own authentic Fabergé someday. Nadine's Fabergé.

The sound of the front door opening prompted Stacey to snap off the television. She smoothed her hair as she moved from her office to the showroom.

Stacey could see past the woman who stood framed in the large picture window. A silver Mercedes sports coupe was parked out front. Stacey put on her brightest smile.

"Can I help you?"

As the woman explained that she was new to town and had just purchased a colonial on Winters Way, dollar signs danced in Stacey's head. Checking their respective diaries, they made an appointment for Stacey to take a look at the woman's new house.

"Let me ask you something," the new client said, as she stopped at the shop door on her way out. "I've lived in Manhattan all my life—doesn't it get a little scary out here? Everything seems so secluded. So isolated." The woman appeared to shiver.

"No," said Stacey, shaking her head from side to side. "The police are wonderful and patrol like mad and just about everyone I know has an alarm system." Stacey lowered her voice to a stage whisper. "But I'll tell you a little secret," she said conspiratorially, wanting the woman to like her.

"I do have my own personal protection."

Chapter 71

"Farrell isn't in the office right now. May I take a message for her?"

"I'm returning her call."

"Is this in reference to a piece she's working on?"

"Yes."

"The art forgery story?"

"With whom am I speaking?" asked Special Agent McCord.

"This is B. J. D'Elia. I'm working with Farrell on the story."

"Okay. Would you please tell her that Jack McCord at the FBI returned her call?"

"I'll see that she gets the message." Dean Cohen lied again as he put the receiver back in its cradle.

Chapter 72

Thursday

Farrell figured that shooting some video at the Metropolitan Museum's Romanov exhibit was a good idea. If and when she could piece together enough information to go with the Moon Egg story, elements from the Russian exhibit would really add to the texture of the package she would produce.

While B. J. fiddled with his camera gear,

Farrell strode through the airy, high-ceilinged gallery rooms, scanning their contents for the items she wanted shot. She stared at a large portrait of the children of Nicholas and Alexandra: the four lovely Romanov daughters and their younger brother, Alexei, the hemophiliac heir to the doomed throne. Their expressions were innocent, trusting, mercifully unaware of the violent fate that awaited them.

Another painting, one of the czar and his beloved czarina, haunted Farrell. Here was the man who had commissioned the Moon Egg as his wife's Easter gift all those years ago. On the other side of the world, the action of the Russian emperor decades before was now impacting on Farrell's life. And the lives of others.

A large, white ostrich-feather fan, part of a costume worn to a Winter Palace ball. Satin gowns covered with diamonds, emeralds, and sapphires. Mother-of-pearl opera glasses, bronze swords encrusted with rubies. Religious objects, icons and altar crosses and golden chalices. And jewelry: pendants and brooches and tiaras and bracelets that had adorned the Romanovs as they ruled Russia for three centuries, wearing pounds of yellow and blue and white diamonds, Ceylon sapphires, and blood-red rubies—while eighty percent of their country's people were living in poverty. The peasant farmers toiled in the impoverished countryside, and the factory workers slaved away in miserable city slums. Russia was ripe for revolution.

As Farrell and B. J. made their way around the exhibit, museumgoers watched them, interested in observing what the television people were doing. A tall, well-coifed woman approached Farrell.

"Excuse me. Didn't I see you recently in the Consignment Depot in New Jersey?"

Startled, Farrell studied the woman's vaguely familiar face, trying to place it. It was the woman who had come into the shop that day with Victor Paradise.

"Stacey Spinner," the woman prompted. "Small world, isn't it?"

"Oh, yes. I remember you now. Nice to see you again—although Pat didn't really get the chance to introduce us. Are you a Romanov fan?" Farrell asked politely.

"Well, yes, I am interested in Russian history," Stacey nodded, "but I especially came to see the Fabergé eggs. This is the largest collection of the Imperial Easter Eggs ever assembled, you know."

"So I hear. Which one do you think is the most interesting?" Might as well get some input from the woman on the street.

"My favorite is the Pansy Egg. I think the surprise inside, the tiny, heart-shaped frames with the miniatures of the Imperial children along with their parents, aunts, and uncles, is quite remarkable."

"We'll make sure to get over there and get a shot of it, then," said Farrell.

"I didn't get *your* name that day in the Consignment Depot."

"Farrell Slater."

"And what exactly do you do, if you don't mind my asking."

Would this woman ever go away? "I'm a producer for KEY News."

"Wow! That must be interesting." Stacey was truly impressed. "And you're doing a story on this exhibit?"

"Actually," snapped Farrell, losing patience, "we're doing a piece on art forgeries."

The moment the words were out of her mouth, Farrell wished she had not blurted out her assignment to a woman she did not even know.

Chapter 73

Long after Eliza Blake had signed off, removed her anchor's mike and gone home, and all of the stage crew had cleared from the *Evening Headlines* studio, Range Bullock sat alone at his desk in the Fishbowl and stared at the latest ratings printout. KEY News was down.

In Range's mind, there was one main reason for the ratings slip. Money. Or rather, the absence of it.

At every one of an endless series of budget meetings, news division president Yelena Gregory pounded home the message. Keep down the spending. That meant sending fewer correspondents, producers, and camera crews on the road to cover stories, which meant using videotape obtained from affiliates when you could get it, and it meant having little quality control. It meant not going for that extra element if it meant springing for a news crew staying an extra night in a hotel in a faraway city or town. It meant thinking about what a story would cost to cover and measuring it against the story's importance. Good stories were being left uncovered because they were too expensive to produce.

His mind turned to the Fabergé story that Farrell was working on. If she could prove what she suspected was true, it would be a powerful *Evening Headlines* exclusive news piece. The fact that it would all be done in New York, and therefore cost relatively little to produce, made it that much sweeter.

Suddenly Range wanted to see that video of the Fabergé egg again, and he didn't want to wait until tomorrow morning to do it. He'd just go up to Farrell's office, check if it was open, look around and see if he could find the videotape.

But when he got there, Farrell's second-floor office wasn't empty. Dean Cohen was inside, sitting at Farrell's desk. When Dean looked up and saw Range standing in the doorway watching him, the younger producer's face reddened.

"I just took a call for Farrell and I was leaving her a message," Dean explained.

Range nodded. He walked to the desk and

looked over the tape boxes on the top. Then he checked the tapes that were stacked on the shelves on the wall.

"Can I help with something?" Dean volunteered.

"No . . . I'm just trying to find a videotape Farrell screened for me the other day. . . ." His voice trailed off as he continued his search.

"On what?" Dean tried to sound casual.

"Some art forgery story she's been working on."

Chapter 74

Friday of the Second Week of Lent

Dean Cohen paid for his coffee and bagel at the Station Break checkout. The KEY cafeteria was ridiculed endlessly by the news staffers, yet they ate there frequently. It was convenient, fast, and relatively cheap.

As Dean paused at the condiment counter to grab some paper napkins, he noticed Far-

rell and B. J. occupying one of the cafeteria
booths. Their heads huddled together, Farrell and the cameraman were in the midst of
an intense conversation. Dean wondered if
Farrell had figured out yet that he had intercepted her message from the FBI agent. He
didn't think so.

Dean hurried from the cafeteria and
walked quickly to the elevator that would
carry him up to the second-floor *Evening
Headlines* offices. He wanted to have a few
minutes in the office before Farrell returned.
When the elevator doors opened, Range
Bullock was waiting in the hallway.

"Hiya, Dean. What's happening?"

"Not much yet, boss, but the day is young."

"Isn't that the truth? God knows what today
will bring. Another terrorist bombing or another campaign scandal." Range shook his
head. "I'm starting to think I'm getting too old
for all this."

Dean laughed. "I wouldn't go around men-
tioning that to other people here, Range. But
your secret is safe with me."

The two men chuckled as Range got into
the elevator Dean had vacated. "By the way,
buddy, it's about time for you to be coming
up with another 'KEYhole,' piece, isn't it?"

"Don't worry, Range. I'm working on something now. I'll let you know when it comes together more."

Range gave a thumbs-up sign as the elevator doors closed. Dean smiled but groaned inwardly. He didn't really have anything he was working on for "KEYhole to America", the lengthy, investigative end-pieces that closed *Evening Headlines* each night. With the exception of the lead story, "KEYholes" were the most coveted assignments on the broadcast. All the producers kept a running mental tally of who had come up with the most "KEYhole" pieces. Dean had been on a streak for a while, but lately his mental well had been running dry.

You're only as good as your last story.

Back in his office, Dean headed straight for Farrell's desk. Again he read her doodle.

Olga. Egg. Video. Fire.

Dean reached for the black metal hide-a-key case that he knew she kept magnetized to the bottom of the desk. His hands trembled as he slid open the case and pulled the small, shiny aluminum key from its bed.

By the time Farrell arrived, minutes later, the videotape of Olga's Moon Egg was snug inside Dean's briefcase.

Chapter 75

It was not unusual for Meryl to work on Saturdays when special auctions were coming up. It was unusual for her to get phone calls from the FBI on the weekend.

"Ms. Quan, the list you provided me of Fabergé consignors and customers has a glaring omission," Special Agent McCord said sternly.

Meryl was intimidated by McCord's menacing tone. "How can I help you, Mr. McCord?"

"You can help me by getting me the name of the person who consigned the Moon Egg for sale to Churchill's."

"That wasn't on the list?"

"Ms. Quan, please don't play innocent with me and don't insult me. No. The name wasn't on the list. And if Churchill's doesn't hand it over, I'm going to get paper and force you to."

Meryl's mind raced. A subpoena would be easy enough for McCord to get. Why hadn't Clifford included the name on the list he had her turn over to the FBI? It just looked like he was hiding something. Was Clifford trying to buy time?

"I'll speak to Mr. Montgomery and see what I can find out, Mr. McCord."

"I'd appreciate it if you do it sooner than later, Ms. Quan. I'll expect a call from you."

The phone line went dead, leaving Meryl worried. The FBI usually ended up getting what it wanted. She didn't want to get on the wrong side of Jack McCord.

Meryl knocked on Clifford's door. The catalogue for the auction of the Nadine Paradise Collection was on Montgomery's desk and her boss was flipping through the thick, glossy pages. Leaf after leaf featured the mementos collected over the years of the ballerina's colorful life. The items for sale had been carefully photographed to show them off to the best advantage. Colorful antique posters from the Ballet Russe, programs from the famous Paradise performances, satin ballet shoes in palest pinks and flaming magentas, hand-engraved sheet music and set-design sketches, costumes

Paradise wore as Aurora in *Sleeping Beauty* and Odele in *Swan Lake.* . . .

It was a coup to acquire the Paradise collection for auction. It would be worth a small fortune to Churchill's in commissions and publicity.

"We have some beautiful things to be sold for her next week, Meryl. I'm so pleased that we are hosting the Paradise auction of her wonderful ballet memorabilia. It ties in so perfectly with our Russian month. And the publicity department tells me that we are getting lots of calls from the media about covering our celebrity auction. That's great exposure."

Clifford looked satisfied and a lot less worried than Meryl had seen him in recent days. She hated to ruin the mood.

"The FBI just called."

"And?"

"The name of the consignor of the Moon Egg wasn't on the Fabergé list we turned over."

"It wasn't?"

"Not according to Agent McCord. He wants it as soon as possible or he's going to go for a subpoena to get it."

Clifford continued to look unruffled. "I'll take care of it," he said.

Meryl remained standing in front of Montgomery's desk.

"Is there something else, Meryl?"

"As a matter of fact, there is," Meryl began uncertainly. "This Moon Egg thing is really bothering me. First KEY News comes in with suspicions about it. Now, the FBI is clearly looking into this, and I'm being called about it. I'm worried that if there is some sort of problem or impropriety that occurred here, it might look like I'm involved."

Clifford studied Meryl, but didn't say anything.

Meryl summoned up the courage to continue. "What I'm trying to say, Clifford, is that I think . . . well, I don't think we can continue to ignore the media and the FBI. Agent McCord is waiting for a return phone call and I seem to be caught in the middle of all this."

Only a tiny vein throbbing at his temple betrayed Clifford's annoyance.

"I said I'd take care of it," he said curtly. Clifford then made a deliberate effort to soften his tone. "Meryl, dear, please don't worry. You aren't in the middle of this at all.

Churchill's guaranteed confidentiality to the buyer and seller, and the entire sale rests on our ability to keep that promise. You will be perfectly safe—as long as you keep out of it."

Chapter 76

Third Sunday of Lent

The sound of Olga's breathing beneath her oxygen mask echoed through the silent hospital room as Farrell and Pat sat quietly next to her bed.

"I try to get here every day," Pat whispered. "I like to think she knows I'm here."

"They say that a coma victim is aware on some level of what is going on around her." Farrell tried to reassure her friend. "I'm sure having your energy here, caring about her, helps Olga."

The two women stared at the frail figure lost in the vastness of the hospital bed. They kept their worried thoughts to themselves as the nurse's aide rustled in to check Olga's vitals and register them in her medical chart.

Pat broke the silence again. "It's so good of you, Farrell, to come out here like this. You've been a real friend."

"It's the least I can do."

"You don't even know Olga."

Farrell wanted to spill out her worries, tell Pat the truth about the Moon Egg and how she had come out and taped it just before the fire. Instead, she honored her promise to Peter. He would have to tell his mother himself.

When they rose to leave, Farrell asked if Pat wanted to go out and grab a bite to eat.

"That would be fun," Pat replied. "But I have a business call I have to make."

"On Sunday?"

"Yep. I'm at the Consignment Depot the rest of the week and on Saturdays. So I have to do my other business at night or on Sundays."

"Well, how about if I come with you and we can get some supper after that? Then I'll take the bus back to Manhattan."

As they walked down the corridor, they met up with Charlie Ferrino. Pat introduced the deli owner to Farrell.

"It's really good of you to come and visit Olga, Charlie," Pat said, reaching out to touch his arm.

"I have a soft spot for the old gal. I'm really pulling for her, but it's not looking so good, is it?"

"Not really." Pat shook her head and smiled weakly.

Farrell and Pat continued down the hallway.

"Did you see the way that guy looked at you, Pat?" Farrell whispered. "He's got it bad."

"Charlie?" Pat laughed incredulously. "He's just the sweet guy at the deli—we've known each other for years."

"I'm telling you, he's crazy about you," Farrell insisted.

Pat's Volvo pulled out of the hospital parking lot onto Old Hook Road, and headed through Westwood, up the steep Washington Avenue hill toward Saddle River. Farrell watched as the more modest houses on small lots gradually led to larger and larger homes on acres of wooded property. When their car pulled into the circular driveway in front of the Tudor mansion, Farrell let out a soft whistle.

"Who lives here?"

"Nadine Paradise."

"The ballerina?"

"Yes. The legend. And the mother of one Victor Paradise who came to the Consignment Depot with Stacey Spinner and so charmingly demanded that I tell him where the crescent brooch that his mother bought at Churchill's came from."

Farrell stared at Pat. "It came from Olga, didn't it?"

Pat nodded silently. "So now Nadine Paradise is going to try to convince me to tell her the pin's provenance. She just about begged me to come to the house today."

"Are you going to tell her?"

"I'm not sure."

 Chapter 77

Leading them just past the small library into the conservatory, Nadine waved Pat and Farrell beyond the baby grand piano, toward two Burmese rattan armchairs with brightly flowered cushions that sat at angles to a matching loveseat. In the center of the tri- angle was an oblong table with brass finish- ings on which a porcelain tea service took up almost all of the space.

The room was not unoccupied. Farrell ob- served that Victor Paradise looked distinctly awkward in a room filled with delicate plants and fine china. He stood up and moved to- ward his mother and the two visitors.

Nadine made the introductions. "You re- member my son, Mrs. Devereaux. Victor, this is Miss Slater, a friend of Mrs. Dever- eaux's." As the women took their seats, Na- dine looked in her son's direction and said, "Victor, dear, would you be kind enough to get us some napkins? If there aren't any on the wet bar in the library, you may have to look in the dining room."

Victor knew he was being dismissed. He walked out of the room as his mother began to pour out her story. Although Mrs. Para- dise directed most of it to Pat, Farrell listened intently to the aged ballerina's rec- ollections and watched her with a television producer's eye for detail.

"So you see," Nadine finished, "I have to know who you sold the crescent brooch for.

I'm convinced that that person has some sort of connection to me. My father, a father I never met and longed for all my life, made that pin for my mother."

Farrell studied the old woman's face, still beautiful in the late-winter sun streaming through the conservatory window. In passing, one would see very little resemblance between the face of this wealthy, artfully made-up legend, and the wrinkled old lady who slept in a hospital bed a few miles away. But as she watched Nadine's expressive hands, they looked familiar, like the delicate ones that lay folded on the blue cotton hospital blanket. Artful hands, hands that could have been part of the genetic code of a workmaster in the Fabergé studio.

Farrell looked over at Pat, who was considering Nadine's appeal. What would it hurt to tell her that the crescent pin was Olga's? Since Olga lay dying, this could be Nadine Paradise's last chance to make peace with her past.

The same thought must have been running through Pat's mind.

"Mrs. Paradise," said Pat gently, "a very sick woman is lying near death at Pascack

Valley Hospital right now. The crescent brooch was hers. Her father made it."

Nadine listened silently but wide-eyed as Pat told her what she knew of Olga's history. The early years in St. Petersburg, defined by the revolution and the death of her mother. Her proud father, once a Fabergé workmaster, left brokenhearted and unable to leave his mother country. Olga's ultimate escape from the Soviet Union and emigration to the United States, her quiet life in Westwood financed by slowly selling off pieces of her father's artistry.

"It's all falling into place. Olga may be my half-sister." Nadine's eyes glistened with tears. "I need some time to take this in."

"Of course."

Victor cleared his throat as he entered the conservatory with three white linen cocktail napkins in his hand. "You were right, Mother," he lied. "I had to look for them in the dining room. I hope I haven't kept you from your tea."

"We were just leaving," said Pat. "We need to get going." She and Farrell rose, and Mrs. Paradise escorted them past her son and out to the foyer.

"What a beautiful scarf." Pat admired a luxurious turquoise scarf left casually on the hallway table. Nadine picked it up and pressed it into Pat's hands.

"Please take it, my dear," she urged.

"But I couldn't," Pat protested.

"Please, I insist. Keep it as a reminder of a day you made an old woman deeply happy."

Chapter 78

Monday

Days had gone by since she'd made the call to Jack McCord and still she hadn't heard back from him. First thing Monday morning, Farrell resolved to call him again. She waited until Dean was out of their office.

"Thanks for the call back," Farrell sniffed sarcastically. "I really feel that my country's security is in capable and efficient hands."

"I did call you back," McCord protested. "Your colleague told me he would give you the message that I returned your call. It

sounds to me like KEY News is the ineffi-
cient organization here."

"I didn't get your message. Did you get the
name of the person with whom you left it?"

"Some guy with initials for a name." Jack
shuffled through some papers on his desk.
"B. J.?"

"Yeah. That's it. B. J. D'Elia. I have it right
here in my notes. He said he was working
the Fabergé story with you."

*It's not like B. J. to neglect giving a mes-
sage,* Farrell thought. *And he's not usually
in my office when I'm not there.* She'd have
to ask him about it later.

"Well, what was it you wanted to talk to me
about?" Agent McCord asked.

Without naming names, Farrell told him
about her suspicions regarding the fire at
Olga's.

"So, let me get this straight. You harass
some old lady and get her to let you take
pictures of her illegal property and she ends
up in a coma somewhere after her apartment catches fire."

Farrell winced. "Yeah. That's about it.
That, and the fact that the woman lived in
fear and, at the same time, her apartment
door was unlocked at the time of the fire."

"Don't you think it's about time you gave me her name and address?"

"I can't."

"Can't, or won't?"

Farrell thought quickly. Without too much trouble, Jack could have the FBI computers check every reported fire that had occurred in the country during any given period. As he checked further, eventually he would end up with the Westwood fire chief, who would willingly give up Olga's identity to the mighty feds.

Maybe, by giving McCord the information he asked for, Farrell could buy a little allegiance from the guy. When the time came he had something to share about his Fauxbergé investigation with the public, maybe he'd choose Farrell to share with, seeing as she had helped him out along the way.

She told him.

"Thanks," he answered matter-of-factly.

"Your gratitude is overwhelming," Farrell remarked dryly. "At least you can help me with this: What are the possible legal ramifications for Olga once it becomes public that she has the real Moon Egg?"

"Well . . ." Jack considered. "This isn't a 'spoils of war' issue. The Russian Revolution was a civil war, not a war between two sovereign countries. But if the Russians find out that Olga has an Imperial Easter Egg looted from the St. Petersburg Fabergé studios back in 1917, they could put a claim in United States Federal Court. A judge would decide its ownership."

"How likely is that scenario?"

"Remote. Plus, from what you tell me, that's the least of the old gal's problems."

Chapter 79

Robbie Slater sat with his sister in a corner booth at the Station Break.

"Man, I can't believe how hard it is for a guy to have lunch with his sister." His cardboard lunch tray held a fat roast-beef sandwich, a package of Fritos, an orange soda, and three packs of Oreos.

"Nice, healthy lunch there, Rob." Farrell nodded as she poked at her plastic salad bowl full of lettuce, tuna salad, and carrot sticks. Farrell noticed with a twinge that his hairline had receded a little more from the last time she saw him. His exposed forehead looked so vulnerable to Farrell.

"You're just jealous. Watching your girlish figure, huh? Somebody new in your life? Is that what's keeping you from returning my calls? Come to think of it, you look especially good today."

"Nah. Same old, same old, but I *have* been busy." Farrell did not want to talk about Jack McCord or fill Robbie in on Olga's fire and the Moon Egg. She especially did not want to tell him yet that she was being let go from KEY News. She did not want him to worry.

"What are you so busy with?" Robbie asked, taking another large bite from his sandwich.

"A story on art forgery. I'd like to develop it into a 'KEYhole to America' piece."

Farrell wanted to change the subject. "How's it going for you, Robbie?"

"Pretty well. I like my job at the tape library. I can't believe all the material that comes in. It's amazing to me how much is shot on each story and how comparatively little makes air. It's fun to look at the outtakes, too. Plus, no one really bugs me over there.

I work at my own pace and that seems to be fine with my boss."

"That's because you're so smart and do a great job, and he knows he's lucky to have you." Farrell always tried to boost Robbie's shaky self-esteem.

"Spoken like my big sister."

"It's true," Farrell protested.

"I think it's more like my boss realizes that for the modest salary they're paying, they can't expect too much, or complain too much."

"Don't sell yourself short, Robbie, please," Farrell pleaded. "I hate when you do that."

Robbie glanced at the large white clock and piled his sandwich wrapper and empty soda can on his tray. He slid the remaining uneaten package of Oreos into his shirt pocket.

"Gotta get back," he said, reaching out to squeeze Farrell's shoulder. "And do me a favor, will you? Stop worrying about me."

Chapter 80

"I was wondering if I could possibly come in for a tour. I've been to the public rooms of Churchill's so many times for exhibitions and auctions, but I'm curious to see what goes on behind the scenes."

Balancing the telephone receiver on her shoulder, Meryl checked her DayTimer. A half-hour of her day was well spent on someone who could help Churchill's. Being polite and accommodating was good for future business at the auction house.

"Of course, I'd be happy to show you around. When would be a good time for you?" Meryl asked.

"I know it's short notice, but you wouldn't happen to have some time tomorrow, would you?"

Meryl scanned her calender. "As a matter of fact, I do have some time open tomor-

row afternoon. How would three o'clock
be?"

"Wonderful. I'll see you then."

Meryl penciled in the appointment.

❧ Chapter 81

Still, she breathed. In and out. In and out.
The clear plastic oxygen mask covered her
nose and mouth.

It was surprising that such an ancient, wizened old thing could hang on so tenaciously.
You had to give the old girl that much. She
didn't want to die.

But there was consolation in the fact that
the nurses looked so glum when they came
in to check on her, the rueful, understanding
smiles they gave to the regular visitor who
kept watch so patiently.

"So many of our elderly patients have no
visitors. It's nice to see someone on in years
get so much company," the blond night
nurse said.

Olga, Olga, Olga. Why don't you let go, sweetheart, make the decision to move on yourself? It would be better that way. Go willingly rather than be forced.

❦ Chapter 82

Tuesday

Farrell was more than a little anxious about Jack McCord coming over to KEY News to take a look at the Moon Egg video. She'd taken care putting on her makeup and dressing this morning, choosing her charcoal-colored Calvin Klein suit, sheer black hose, and stack-heeled pumps.

"What's the occasion?" B. J. asked when he saw Farrell in the hallway.

"Can't I dress up a little without it being an occasion?"

"No."

She waved him off and continued on her way. Then she stopped and turned back in B. J's direction.

"Hey, hot shot," she called. "Thanks for giving me my message."

B. J looked puzzled.

"The message from the FBI agent," she prompted.

"Since when do I take messages for you?"

"You didn't take a message for me from Jack McCord at the FBI?"

"Not me, kiddo. Must have been someone else."

Chapter 83

Holding open Churchill's door, Tony greeted the visitor by name.

The coat checked, the visitor was announced by the Churchill's security staffer at the front desk in the lobby.

"Ms. Quan will be right down," he said.

"Thank you."

The visitor paced back and forth. Waiting.

Meryl Quan descended the stairs, her hand extended. "How good to see you again. I thought we'd start upstairs with the various offices, Business Department, Trusts and Estates, et cetera. Then we'll work our way down to the jewelry gallery and the board of directors' conference room. We'll finish up by going backstage, where the storage rooms are. That's where the items that are going to be auctioned are kept. Our security department is also situated back there."

"Great."

Meryl guided the visitor, floor by floor, through the labyrinth of Churchill's offices, explaining the function of each.

"Fascinating," the visitor said, eyes observing the security cameras positioned in the halls and doorways.

"This is my favorite part of the tour," said Meryl. "Backstage where the work is done to ready the items for auction." Meryl led the way through a maze of storerooms where shelves held auction items according to category. Furniture, bronzes, silver and glass, rugs. . . . Each room had cameras peeking from various points in the ceiling. The visitor's heart was sinking.

"My Lord, what's all that?" An opened door revealed an organized jumble of what looked like space suits.

"Those are items for the Russian Space History Sale. It's rather sad, really—they're selling off their history just to survive financially. . . . And here is our security area," said Meryl as they moved on. A guard sat at the console, watching three dozen television screens that covered the wall in front of him. "As you can see, we are very careful here."

The visitor nodded. "Impressive."

"That about wraps up our tour. Is there anything else I can show you?" Meryl offered.

"No, I think I've seen all I was interested in seeing."

"Then let me walk you out." Meryl escorted the visitor from the security room and down the hallway toward the public area. They stopped momentarily, blocked by two moving-men who were unloading a heavy, tiger-oak dining table from an oversized freight elevator.

The freight elevator. It had no camera!

Chapter 84

When Farrell went to greet Jack in the Broadcast Center lobby, she noticed with satisfaction that he thirstily drank in her appearance. Farrell was glad that she'd made the extra effort as Jack shook her hand firmly and his piercing blue eyes locked onto hers.

"I'm glad you've decided to share your information with us, Farrell."

So now it was Farrell instead of Ms. Slater. Good sign.

"Well, the fire at Olga's really changed things from my perspective. I'm afraid someone is playing for keeps here, and I don't want anyone else to get hurt. Let's stop in my office. I'll get the videotape from my desk and I have a viewing room reserved for us."

"I'm surprised big-shot network news producers have to share offices," said Jack, gesturing toward Dean Cohen's empty desk.

"Yeah. I'm not only surprised, but unhappy, too. It's not that I have a need to work alone—most of my work is out in the field anyway. There's just not enough space in the Center for all the broadcasts that are being worked on here. KEY News has expanded a lot since the time we moved into this building."

Farrell unlocked her desk drawer and reached for the videotape B. J. had shot. At first puzzled, and then frantic, she emptied the drawer searching for the tape.

"Don't tell me," Jack said cynically. "It's not there."

"It's got to be here. Maybe I put it in another drawer."

Soon the entire contents of Farrell's desk were strewn out on the top. No videotape. Where was it? She was embarrassed in front of the no-nonsense FBI agent.

Jack, though, didn't seem overly concerned. "Hopefully it'll turn up. Why don't you just tell me exactly what Olga showed you?"

Farrell described for him the yellow velvet carrying case, inscribed with the Cyrillic letters, enough of which she could recognize as spelling Fabergé. She told of Olga's opening the case and taking from it the milk-colored, enamel-and-gold egg that rested on a cloud of midnight-blue stone.

"Lapis lazuli?" he asked.

"Yes, that's what I think it's called. I was at the Moon Egg auction, Jack. Olga's egg looks just like the egg at Churchill's. Except for one thing. Olga's had the surprise still intact inside the egg. The auctioned one, as you know, did not."

"What was the surprise?"

"A spray of diamonds. Brilliant diamonds. Olga called them a comet. I admit that I'm no expert, but I'd bet the farm those diamonds were real."

Jack made some notations in his notebook.

Farrell folded her arms across her chest. "Well, what do you think?"

"I've seen the design plans for the Fabergé Moon Egg, Farrell. The surprise called for a comet of diamond stars, signifying Halley's Comet which appeared in the early part of the century. From what you are describing to me, my gut tells me that you've seen the real Moon Egg."

"Now what?"

"Now I think you should leave this case to

the professionals. Obviously you are tread-
ing dangerous waters here."

Farrell smiled. "Know what I think?"

"I know you are going to tell me whether I
want to hear it or not."

"You're right. I think two heads are better
than one, and that if we work together, we
can solve this thing. You'd get kudos at the
FBI, and I would score big around here.
Sounds good, doesn't it?"

"If you really want to know the truth, Farrell, I'd be a lot more interested in having
dinner with you than in working with you on
a case."

"That's what you think now, Jack. You
might find out, though, that both scenarios
will be mutually satisfying."

Chapter 85

The Nadine Paradise auction was worth a pitch. Viewers were interested in celebrity auctions, loved the vicarious thrill of peeking into famous people's personal lives. Farrell herself remembered going to the Duke and Duchess of Windsor auction preview at Sotheby's and being mesmerized at finding the Elizabeth Arden recipe for the duchess's black hair dye, the hundreds of gloves the duchess wore because she was self-conscious about her large hands, and a box with a piece of the couple's 1937 wedding cake.

Farrell was certain that she could do a fascinating piece on the Paradise collection. She could shoot the most interesting items for sale at the preview over the coming days, and Friday she could cover the auction itself. The piece would air on *Evening Headlines* on Friday night.

As she tapped out her note to Range on her computer, Farrell was grateful for e-mail. It gave her a chance to compose and express her thoughts without having the uncomfortable pressure of having to pass her idea by Range face-to-face.

Go for it, came the executive producer's e-mailed reply.

Yes! thought Farrell. The Paradise auction was a cool story, but even more important to her, it was another opportunity to get over to Churchill's.

Chapter 86

Thursday

The elegant woman, cloaked in a jacket of brown broadtail fur with braid edging, carried a small matching muff as she alighted from the black Mercedes sedan in front of Churchill's. Though passersby did not immediately identify her, they instinctively sensed that the woman was "somebody."

"I'll park the car, Mother, and I'll meet you inside."

"Thank you, Victor dear."

The Churchill's doorman, a welcoming smile on his face, held the door open wide for Nadine Paradise, who stopped for a moment to talk with him.

"How have you been, Tony?"

"Just fine, Mrs. Paradise."

"Holding up with all the Russian festivities?"

"Yes, ma'am."

Nadine eyed the cossack costume and an idea struck her. "You know, Tony, I think I'd like to see you inside during my auction tomorrow. Do you think you could come inside and stand in your uniform next to the auction platform? I think that would be a nice touch."

"Certainly, Mrs. Paradise. Whatever you and Mr. Montgomery want."

Nadine pressed a crisp bill into the doorman's hand.

"Good to see you, Tony."

"Thank you, Mrs. Paradise."

Clifford Montgomery and Meryl Quan were waiting inside for Nadine, and welcomed her warmly.

"I hope you will be quite pleased with our

display of your wonderful things, Mrs. Paradise," Clifford said solicitously. "We are so happy to have the opportunity to showcase these treasures."

The threesome entered the busy auction gallery, alive with the energy of the interested public inspecting—and television crews filming—the relics of Nadine's ballet career. Mural-sized blowups of decades-old pictures of Nadine dancing *The Firebird, Scheherazade*, and *The Rite of Spring* hung on the gallery walls, serving as a backdrop for the carefully arranged items that would soon be auctioned. Spotlights illuminated framed water-colored costume sketches and set-design plans that were works of art in themselves. The jeweled and feathered headpieces that had once crowned Nadine's head as she pirouetted on the stages of the world, now hung on Churchill's walls, waiting to be taken home by the highest bidder.

"Clifford, you've done a beautiful job here."

"Thank you, Mrs. Paradise."

Nadine continued her tour, satisfied with the decision to divest herself of all these things. It would be that much less for Victor to do after she was gone.

"Excuse me, Mrs. Paradise?"

"Miss Slater! It's so nice to see you here."

"Thank you for remembering me. I'm here covering the auction for KEY News. I was wondering if you'd be willing to be interviewed briefly."

"Certainly, dear."

Clifford Montgomery was clearly annoyed. Meryl tried to hide her pleasure at seeing B. J. approach with his camera, while Victor Paradise arrived at his mother's side.

Farrell started with some questions about Nadine's dance career, asking her if there were any auction items that were of particular significance. Nadine answered eloquently, her French accent giving her responses an almost melodious quality. Farrell knew that, back in the editing room, she would have good material to work with.

"Why now, Mrs. Paradise? Why did you decide to auction these things off now?" Farrell asked.

Nadine smiled. "As one gets older, one wants to simplify one's life. This just felt like the right time to let go of a few things and move on." She failed to mention that the money would be welcome income after living so many years in retirement.

Chapter 87

Friday of the Third Week of Lent

You had to hand it to them. Churchill's really knew how to do it right.

Farrell observed and B. J. shot as the Paradise auction began. Clifford Montgomery made brief opening remarks from the auctioneer's platform. The lights dimmed and a movie screen lowered from the ceiling. As the music of Tchaikovsky and Stravinsky played, black-and-white slides of the prima ballerina flickered on the screen.

When the lights came back up and the applause died down, a Russian cossack appeared to stand guard as the first item for sale wheeled into view on the automated platform. The costume that Nadine Paradise wore in the title role of *The Firebird.* Farrell consulted her auction catalogue to read that the ballet was based on a selection of Russian fairy stories. It was a good selection to start off another auction in Churchill's Russian series.

Farrell was really beginning to feel comfortable at the auction house—not feeling, as she once had that it was a hushed, intimidating place that only the very, very wealthy dared enter. As she looked around the gallery, she saw faces she recognized. Nadine Paradise, of course, and her son Victor. Farrell was interested to see that Stacey Spinner was sitting with them.

Where was Pat? Farrell wondered. She had said that she was going to close up the Consignment Depot and come to the auction with Tim Kavanagh.

Farrell felt a tap on her shoulder, and her spine stiffened.

"We have to stop meeting like this."

It was Jack.

"They really do let just about anyone in here, don't they?" Farrell whispered. Suddenly the auction had become even more stimulating.

Chapter 88

"I'm interested in something that's going to be auctioned at the Russian Space History Sale, and I won't be able to make it to the preview. Can you show it to me?"

"Right now?" asked Meryl.

"I know it's an imposition, but I don't have much time."

Meryl glanced around the auction gallery. Everything was going smoothly. It wouldn't hurt if she slipped away for a few minutes.

Meryl led the way. "I hope you don't mind, but we have to take the freight elevator."

"I don't mind in the least."

Did the costumed doorman look in their direction? Couldn't be sure.

It had to be quick. There was no time for any more bungling.

As the freight elevator doors closed behind them, Meryl drew in a sharp breath as she felt something snap around her neck. She struggled urgently but silently as she tried to rip away whatever it was that was choking her. She fought hard, but the strong hands that twisted the tourniquet around her neck were unrelenting.

When it was over, Meryl's limp body collapsed. Although the deadweight was heavy, the corpse was easily folded and stuffed into the large packing barrel at the side of the freight elevator. Forcefully the barrel was clamped shut, as a Hermès scarf slipped through the narrow opening at the side of the car and wafted down the elevator shaft.

Chapter 89

B. J. looked for Meryl before he and Farrell left Churchill's. He had wanted to confirm their date for Saturday night but he couldn't find her. Farrell had been anxious to get back to the Broadcast Center to start putting her auction story together and B. J. had wanted to get back to check the quality of the tape he'd shot.

He thought he'd gotten some good stuff, and his hunch was confirmed as he played the videotapes back for Farrell.

"Nice work," she said. "I notice you got some good shots of your girlfriend as well."

B. J. grinned. "You know what they say— all work and no play. . . ."

"Get out of here, you goofball. I have work to do." Farrell opened up a new computer page to begin composing her story.

"In another of the growing phenomenon known as celebrity auctions, the collection of the renowned ballerina Nadine Paradise went on sale today at Churchill's in New York City, attracting an audience eager to pay to have a piece of a legend's life. . . ."

She typed for the next forty-five minutes, interweaving her writing with sound bites from Nadine Paradise and from three of the enthusiastic auctiongoers she had inter-viewed today. Farrell glanced at her wrist-watch. Five o'clock. She punched the computer keys to send the script down to Range in the Fishbowl.

Fifteen minutes later, the executive pro-ducer called.

"Drop the third auctiongoer's soundbite, change the close to read, 'Nadine Paradise, who has spent so much of her life on center stage earning the applause and hearts of her admirers, won their fealty again this afternoon at Churchill's.' Then go ahead and track. Eliza Blake will be ready to record in booth three."

With just over an hour until airtime, Farrell made the script adjustments and hurried downstairs to the editing area. She felt satisfied that Range had changed so little of her script. In the past, she had thought he had taken great relish in ripping her work apart.

✖ Chapter 90

Fourth Sunday of Lent

All day Saturday B. J. had tried to reach Meryl, unsuccessfully. Was she giving him a none-too-subtle message that she did not want to go out with him anymore?

Saturday night, he had left another message on her answering machine at home: "Meryl, it's Beej. Please call me, honey. I'm worried sick about you."

With pages of the Sunday *Daily News* spread out over his bed, B. J. decided to try her at Churchill's. Maybe she had work to catch up on after the auction on Friday. His heart leapt as the phone was picked up on the second ring.

"Clifford Montgomery." The voice sounded anxious.

"Hi, I'm trying to reach Meryl Quan."

"Who's calling, please?"

"B. J. D'Elia. I'm a friend of hers. We had plans for last night and I haven't been able to reach her. I was hoping she would be there at the office."

"I wish she were, Mr. D'Elia. I haven't seen Meryl since Friday afternoon at the auction here. I've been calling her at home myself. It's not at all like her to just disappear like this. Not when we have another important auction we're preparing for. She is really very conscientious."

B. J.'s heart pounded fearfully. "I'm calling the police."

Chapter 91

Monday

Farrell walked to work, anxious and tense about B. J.'s frantic call the night before. First Olga; now Meryl. Where was she? She didn't want to admit it to herself, but she was frightened.

Dean was waiting for her when Farrell arrived in their office.

"I was in the Fishbowl Friday night when your piece on the Paradise auction ran. Range loved it."

"That must have made you very happy, Dean," Farrell snapped back sarcastically.

"Whoa. Sorry. I just thought I'd pass on a little good news for a change. I'll be sure not to do that again." Dean turned back to his newspaper.

"Cut the crap, Dean. Let's not pretend that you are rooting for me. You'll be glad to have a new officemate. And now that I'm leaving, may I take this opportunity to tell you what a lowlife, sneaky skunk I think you are."

The color rose in Dean's cheeks and he attempted to mount a sputtering protest, but Farrell pressed on.

"Don't play innocent. I know you've intercepted phone calls and purposefully neglected to give me the messages. I know you sniff around my computer and eavesdrop on my phone conversations. And though I can't prove it yet, I know you are the reason why a videotape crucial to a story that could save my career here is missing from my desk."

"Hey, Farrell, don't blame me if you misplaced something."

" 'Misplaced,' my foot! You took it, and don't worry, I'm going to prove that you did. I wonder what your buddy Range will say when I tell him that his boy wonder is a common thief. So much for journalistic integrity!"

"Be careful, Farrell," Dean warned.

"*You* be careful, Dean."

Chapter 92

"Can you believe it?" the overalled stage-hand asked his coworker. "Now we're auctioning off Commie spacesuits, for Christ's sake. Russian Space History Sale, my ass. I'll be glad when this Russian thing is over. I'm sick and tired of getting here so damned early to set up."

"You and me both," agreed his companion. "You gotta feel sorry for those cosmonauts, though. Having to sell off all their space souvenirs just to get some money to live."

"Ah . . . I don't feel sorry for those guys. They worked against us all those years. Now they're getting what they deserve. Their country is a mess."

The stagehands pushed a large dolly stacked with spacesuits, helmets, thick gloves, and parachutes, and stopped to wait for the freight elevator that would carry the merchandise to the gallery above.

"Hey, lookie here, a doggie spacesuit!

Those Russians were big on sending animals into orbit."

The stagehand held up the miniature suit for his friend to see as the elevator doors opened. Instantly both men winced as they inhaled the putrid stench of what they would soon find out was decomposing flesh.

"Oh man, it smells like something died in here."

Chapter 93

Another week gone by, and still no check from Churchill's.

Orchestrating the forgery and the sale of a Fabergé egg was a colossal feat in itself. Now, with the murders of Misha and Meryl, and Olga still to be dealt with, if necessary, that money from the auctioned Moon Egg had been earned many times over. And the work to be done was not finished. Unfortunately, it looked like there were others who were getting in the way and might have to be taken care of as well.

The phone was picked up on the third ring at Churchill's.

"Clifford Montgomery."

"You've taken to answering your own phone?"

"What do you want?"

"My money."

"Listen, while you're sitting safe and sound, I've got the FBI on my back."

"Poor Clifford. If it makes you feel any better, I've been busy, too."

"It doesn't make me feel better. I'm drowning here. Besides, the buyer is having some trouble coming up with the money. And even if I did have it, should I issue a check now, the feds would be all over me."

"Well, you better think of something, bucko. Get the money from that secret buyer of yours or I'll tip off the FBI myself."

Clifford laughed nervously. "You do that, and you'll go down with me."

"You forget, don't you? All I need to say is that I bought the egg at the Twenty-Sixth Street Flea Market and brought it to *you* for authentication. Don't worry, I'll be just as shocked as your buyer that the egg is a fake. There's nothing in the world that can connect me to the forgery."

The auction-house president thought about his career. He was being hung out to dry and he knew it. He wished he had never gotten involved in this. A chance circumstance had led to this nightmare and it was going to take more than mere chance to end it.

"Just get me that money, Clifford. Or you're the one who'll be going to jail. I have the feeling you won't like the accommodations in federal prison. That's where you'll go if I'm forced to make that call."

Chapter 94

Tuesday

"They found Meryl's body." B. J. stood, shell-shocked, in the doorway.

Farrell felt pinned to her chair, dumbfounded.

"Oh, B. J. No. Oh no!"

The cameraman slowly walked to the couch positioned against Farrell's office wall, and sat down heavily. Closing his eyes, he laid his head back against the top of the sofa, and sighed from deep within his chest.

"They found her this morning, in a packing barrel at Churchill's. From the condition of things, they think she was lying there all weekend."

"Oh God, B. J. I'm so sorry."

Farrell sat quietly for a few moments with her friend.

"What are the police saying?"

"The usual. They're investigating, so they aren't saying much. An autopsy will be performed to figure out how she was killed."

Killed. Farrell rubbed the tops of her crossed arms, suddenly cold.

"Do you know anyone who would want to hurt Meryl, Beej?" she asked softly.

But B. J. wasn't listening to Farrell's question. "I just saw her at the auction on Friday. She was so much fun. We were planning to see each other this weekend. If only I had stuck around at Churchill's until I found her, rather than rushing back here to check if my stupid video was good, maybe, just maybe, Meryl would be alive right now."

Farrell rose and sat next to B. J. on the couch, taking his hands in hers.

"Beej, you can't beat yourself up like this. If someone wanted to kill Meryl, he or she would have done it eventually. You couldn't be with her twenty-four hours a day."

"That's for sure," B. J. sneered. "Not the way she lived at that damn auction house, with that boss of hers always giving her *agita*."

"Clifford Montgomery?"

"Yeah. She was worried that Montgomery was into something that she didn't want anything to do with."

❧ Chapter 95

Every month, the elevator maintenance man came to Churchill's to make sure the company's lifts were running well and safely. Liam O'Shea was actually due on the seventeenth of the month, but today he was twenty-four hours early. He wanted to take tomorrow off to go to the St. Patrick's Day parade.

Working in the sub-basement, one by one

Liam checked the motors and wiring of the various elevators, getting, at last, to the freight elevator. At the bottom of the shaft lay what he could tell was a very expensive woman's scarf. *Hermès-Paris* was printed prominently in the design.

Liam thought of turning the scarf in to auction house security. They must run a lost-and-found. But temptation lured. Mary had always wanted a scarf like this one. He had even checked out the prices at Christmas-time last year, planning to splurge and buy his wife something she would never buy for herself. But with three kids in parochial high school, and with college coming up for all of them, he just couldn't rationalize spending $250 for a scarf.

The women who came to Churchill's probably had drawers of scarves, Liam reasoned, when his hardworking Mary had never had anything so fine in all her life. Was that fair?

He packed up his toolbox and carefully folded the silken scarf into a small square which he slipped into his jacket pocket. His Mary would get a St. Patty's Day surprise this year. She deserved it.

Chapter 96

The best thing to do was to get rid of the evidence. But how?

Dean dwelled on Farrell's threat. That was the last thing he needed. A bad reputation. He had carefully cultivated his position on Range's good side. Trying to sabotage Farrell's story wasn't worth jeopardizing his standing with the executive producer.

He didn't want to destroy the videotape. At some point it might be to his advantage to be able to get his hands on it. But Dean didn't want to have it in his actual possession anymore.

Then it occurred to him. He knew where to send it. There it would sit, with thousands of companions, undisturbed and undetected.

Chapter 97

Wednesday, St. Patrick's Day

"If I'd waited for you to ask me to come over for a home-cooked meal, I'd have starved to death. Though I admit, this is some pathetic dinner for St. Patrick's Day. I don't know how to make corned beef and cabbage."

Jack looked at Farrell expectantly, hoping for a flippant answer. But there was none. Farrell twisted the spaghetti around her fork and sipped her wine, unable to stop thinking about the violent death of Meryl Quan.

"Some more merlot?" Jack asked.

Farrell nodded.

"Jack, I've just got this cold, frightened feeling inside. A feeling of impending doom. Someone just walked right into Churchill's and murdered Meryl Quan. Just like I think someone walked right into Olga's apartment and meant to kill her."

"And you think they're connected—how?" Jack prompted.

"Meryl was in the office the day I told Clifford Montgomery my suspicions about the auctioned egg being a forgery. B. J. told me that Meryl said her boss was very upset after my visit." Farrell thought for a moment. "Olga was in possession of the real Fabergé egg that B. J. and I went out to Westwood to shoot just before the fire. Coincidence? I don't think so." Farrell downed the rest of the merlot. "So now we have one murder and one attempted murder."

"Make that two murders."

Farrell looked at him sharply. "How so?"

Jack told Farrell about the vicious murder of Misha in the tiny jewelry workshop in Brighton Beach.

"Did they ever find a body?" asked Farrell.

"Judging from all the blood left behind, if they find anything, it will only be part of a body. Misha Grinkov doesn't exist in one piece anymore."

Farrell stopped to digest what Jack had told her. "Why didn't you tell me all this about Misha before?"

"Before, things seemed fairly removed from you and your safety."

"And now?"

Jack rose from his chair and walked

around the table to her. He pulled her to her feet and led her over to his living-room couch. Taking her face in his hands, he kissed her softly, then firmly on the mouth, and he felt her arms circle willingly around his neck.

"And now?" she whispered again.

"It may not be long before things start getting a bit too close to you."

Chapter 98

Thursday

Every day since Patricia Devereaux had told her the identity of the seller of the crescent brooch, Nadine had had Victor drive her over to Pascack Valley Hospital.

"Come back in about an hour, dear. I'll be waiting for you in the lobby."

Nadine watched as Victor drove off in the Mercedes. He had shown little interest in having anything to do with the sick woman inside who was his newfound aunt. Nadine was disappointed with her son's indifference.

Nadine walked down the long hallway to Olga's room, smiling at the nurse who staffed the desk outside her room. She sat down and began to talk soothingly in Russian to her older sister.

"Please, Olga. Please, dearest one. You must hold on. I've longed for a sister my whole life. And now—now that we finally have a chance to know one another, we cannot lose that gift. I will take good care of you. You can come live with me. I have a big house with plenty of room. Our papa in heaven will be so happy if he knows that his two girls are together at long last."

Nadine took Olga's delicate hand, so like her own, and held it tightly.

"Please, Olga. Please. You must try."

Nadine felt a weak squeeze.

Chapter 99

Farrell stood before Range Bullock's desk and pleaded her case. The executive producer was unmoved.

"As long as you don't have the real Moon Egg, or at least the videotape of it, I don't see how we can go with the story."

"But Range, B. J. and I both saw it with our own eyes, and you yourself saw the video-tape," Farrell pleaded.

Range was shaking his head. He said out loud what Farrell could not bring herself to say. "That's all well and good, but we no longer have any documentable evidence, now, do we?" He paused, and then drove home his point. "With the growing spate of lawsuits against network news divisions recently, you can understand why I am hesitant about sticking our necks out on this story. KEY News does not need a multi-million-dollar defamation suit with Churchill's."

Farrell was not dissuaded. She considered revealing her suspicions about Dean and the missing tape, but thought better of it. Stick to the story. "We're talking about two murders and an attempted murder here."

"Can you prove the murders are related to the Fabergé egg?"

Farrell was silent.

"Look," Range relented slightly. "I'm not saying that this isn't a great story. *If* you can prove it. As it stands now, it's too soft."

"I'm not through with this yet," Farrell resolved as she strode out of the Fishbowl.

Range watched her walk across the studio floor and found himself wishing that Farrell had shown this much tenacity in the months before he had made his decision to let her go.

Chapter 100

Robbie unloaded the latest carton of video-tapes that had arrived via the KEY News traffic desk. It contained a dozen tapes shot at the St. Patrick's Day parade.

Stacking the tapes, he carried them over to his video monitor, and one by one inserted them into the machine, taking computer notes on what was recorded on each tape.

Marching bands, ruddy-faced police officers, bagpipes, and lots and lots of people wearing green. One St. Patty's Day like so many others.

Robbie popped in the seventh tape, fully expecting more of the same. Instead, a very old woman holding a spray of sparkling diamonds appeared on the television monitor.

Chapter 101

Friday of the Fourth Week of Lent

Russian Peasant Folk Belief

*"Whoever fasts on this Friday
will be saved from unjust murder."*

"Please, Olga. Just try to take a little of this broth. It's important so that we can get you off the intravenous feedings," the night nurse urged.

"My throat is sore. I cannot swallow."

"That's from the oxygen," said the nurse. "But now that you're off it, your throat will get better in a few days."

"That is when I eat, then."

The nurse smiled to herself. Tough old cookie. For weeks, no one had thought she was going to make it and now, just over twenty-four hours after coming out of her coma, Olga's stubborn streak was shining through. How strong the human spirit is!

"All right, dear. We'll try again tomorrow. Good night." The nurse smoothed the blanket on the hospital bed and left to tend to her next patient.

Olga lay with her eyes closed, drifting in and out of sleep. The intermittent call of the hospital paging system penetrated her fragmented dreams. *"Ma ijtso. Ma ijtso."*

A visitor leaned close over Olga's sleeping body. "Yes, old soul, 'your egg.' Your egg is the reason you must die."

The visitor's back blocked the view from the doorway. The night nurse, coming back into the room with a fresh pitcher of water, could not see the pillow poised in the visitor's hands. "Isn't it wonderful to see her doing so well?" she chirped to the old woman's frequent guest.

Fluffing the pillow, the visitor turned to smile. "I just want her to be as comfortable as possible.

She's been through so much."

Chapter 102

Charlie was closing up for the night, locking the front door of the deli. Out of habit he looked in the direction of the Consignment Depot. What he made out in the dusk's light made his heart sink.

Pat was walking down the path in front of her shop, accompanied by that guy she had been seeing routinely for several weeks now. Charlie watched as the man opened the car door for her and Pat got inside. Where were they going? What would they do in their next hours together?

You're a fool to let this get to you, he told himself. *You don't know if she really cares about the guy. She isn't being disloyal to you. She doesn't even know how you pine for her. You've never let her know how much you care about her.*

Why haven't you told her? Because you're

afraid, you coward. Afraid that someone like her could never go for someone like you.

Charlie walked to the alley behind the deli and deposited a large, black trash bag into a heavy metal garbage can. He continued to beat himself up. *So now you're going home to spend another Saturday night with the remote control and a six-pack of Budweiser. You've got to do something, man! Make a stand. Just see if there is any way that Pat could possibly care for you—could stop thinking of you like a brother and more like a. . . .*

Maybe if she knew that you had wealth. You've never let her know that you could take care of her, give her a wonderful life, let her quit her job if she wanted. She only thinks of you as Choo-Choo Charlie, the guy with the bald spot covered with a baseball cap, slicing salami and liverwurst at the deli.

No wonder she wasn't impressed.

Chapter 103

Fifth Sunday of Lent

There was still time to get Olga. But doing it at the hospital was out.

Misha, Meryl, and, eventually, Olga. And now, unfortunately, another.

Tony, the Churchill's doorman. He could point a finger. He recognized anyone who came into Churchill's with any regularity. He could name names.

It was uncertain that Tony had noticed anything unusual, dressed in his cossack costume, adding color to the event as he stood guard during the Paradise auction. He might not have been watching as Meryl strode across the gallery to exit down to the storerooms. But he could have been. His eyes seemed to be looking in their direction.

No, it wasn't a certainty, but it was a possibility. A strong possibility that could not be ignored.

Chapter 104

"It's been almost a week, Jack, since they found Meryl's body. What the hell are the police doing?"

"Hey, Farrell, any chance we could just enjoy the first springlike day this year?" Jack popped the other half of his third Krispy Kreme into his mouth.

Farrell and Jack sat on a bench in Strawberry Fields, the Central Park memorial to John Lennon, at West 72nd Street. Across Central Park West, the Gothic Dakota, home to the wealthy, famous, and accomplished, loomed above the trees.

Jack was right. It was a beautiful day, the first tantalizing taste of the spring to come. It had been a rough winter and Farrell was relieved that it was over. But Meryl Quan would not be here to savor the budding trees, the chirping birds, the warm breeze.

Of course, Meryl hadn't expected not to be here, Farrell reflected. She had lived through the previous spring not knowing that it would be her last. Meryl had had every right to think she would have scores of springs to come: riding in convertibles with the tops down; falling in love and watching tulips and daffodils bloom; even getting married and having babies of her own. Meryl had been cheated of all that.

Farrell took Jack's arm and lay her head on his broad shoulder. "God, life is so uncertain," she whispered.

Chapter 105

Tuesday

The treadmills hummed at the coed health spa. Victor and Stacey exercised side by side, Victor running hard, Stacey bouncing at a brisk walk.

"So now Mother wants the old crone to come live with us," Victor puffed.

"Would that be the end of the world?"

"Just what I need, two old ladies to take

care of. As it is, there's something creepy about a guy my age living with his mother. Now I'll be there with two old girls, and you know damn well they're only going downhill from here on in. That means good ol' Victor is going to have to play nursemaid."

Stacey rearranged the terry-cloth sweatband that circled her forehead. "If you're so sure of that, why don't you move out now, while you've got the chance? You're certainly entitled to have a life of your own."

Victor finished running his four miles and waited for Stacey to come to the end of her two-mile power walk. They made their way to the Nautilus machines. Victor lowered himself into the leg press and Stacey stood over him as he adjusted the weights.

"You know, Victor, sooner or later, you are going to be a very wealthy man."

Victor grunted. "But when are you and I finally going to have some real fun?"

Stacey looked around. Everyone seemed to be minding their own business. "Don't get so discouraged all the time," she said. "You've got to be patient. You don't hear me complaining."

"My mother doesn't have as much money

as you think." He hadn't meant to blurt that out.

Stacey took a swig from her water bottle, trying to appear nonchalant.

"What do you mean?"

"Why do you think she sold all that stuff at auction?"

Considering his words, Stacey responded with a lie. "Stop worrying, sweetheart. We'll be okay. I'm on your side, Victor. You know that money has nothing to do with the way I feel about you."

Even Victor was not dumb enough to believe that.

Chapter 106

Farrell walked across the street from the Broadcast Center to the KEY News garage to track down B. J. She wanted to tell him the news in person. Something like this shouldn't be heard over the phone.

B. J. was lying with his feet up on the couch in the crew room, the spot where the union camera guys hung out when they were waiting to be assigned to a story. Empty paper coffee cups and day-old newspapers lay strewn on tables. A soap opera blared from the television bolted to the wall, but B. J. was not watching. He was staring up at the ceiling.

"Hi."

B. J. sat up quickly, surprised to see Farrell.

"Hey, what brings you over to this side of the world?"

Farrell took a place next to B. J. "The autopsy is back."

"And?"

"It shows that Meryl was strangled."

B. J. was quiet for a moment.

"And?"

"From the condition of her body, they figure that she had been dead two to three days before they discovered her."

"How do you know?" he asked.

"Jack McCord told me."

B. J. bowed his head and Farrell knew he didn't want her to see the tears that had come readily to his eyes.

She barely heard him whisper, "If only I'd been there for her."

Chapter 107

"What should I do with this tape, boss?" Robbie asked. "It came in with the St. Patrick's Day tapes but clearly doesn't belong with them."

"What's on it?"

"Shots of an old lady and some kind of jeweled egg."

"Any markings on the tape box?"

"No assignment number or story slug. No cameraman's name, either."

"When are those guys out in the field going to realize how important it is to mark their tapes?" the exasperated supervisor asked. "Just leave it up at the front desk, Rob. Sooner or later someone will probably come looking for it."

Chapter 108

"What are you doing going through my desk?" Dean Cohen demanded.

Unruffled, Farrell looked up from the desk drawer she was rifling through.

"Turnabout is fair play, Dean, my man. Two can play your sneaky little game."

"What the hell are you talking about, Farrell?"

"Where is my videotape?" she demanded.

"I have no idea."

"The hell you don't."

Farrell yanked open the next drawer, continuing her search.

"Stop rummaging through my drawers or I'm going to call security."

"Call away. And I'll tell the guards and anyone else who happens to be walking by and sees all the hubbub, that you, Dean Cohen, are a liar, a sneak, and a thief!"

"You better watch out, Farrell."

"Of course, they may not be sure they can believe me," she said, pulling open another drawer. "But the seeds of doubt will be planted in their minds. It will be my happy legacy to you, dear Dean, that even after I'm gone from the hallowed halls of KEY News, people will look at you and wonder if you really are the dishonest slimeball I said you were. You know how happy news travels around here."

"You're not going to find your tape in my desk, Farrell," Dean said quietly.

"Well, it sure as hell better turn up soon."

Chapter 109

Friday of the Fifth Week of Lent

Inside the cavernous expanse of the United Nations building on New York City's East Side, Professor Tim Kavanagh leaned over the railing with the students he was escorting from Seton Hall University's School of

Diplomacy and International Relations, and watched the giant metal globe sway back and forth on its wire pendulum.

The artist who had designed the moving display had managed to convey a united world.

"Come on, gang. The lecture starts in ten minutes."

Kavanagh led the group of hopeful future diplomats to the auditorium where they were to hear a talk on the history of the UN, and the new trends in diplomacy caused by the realignment of global power structures. Once the students had taken their seats and the UN lecturer had begun, Professor Kavanagh slipped out of the room. He had a good hour and a half to kill before he had to come back.

Chapter 110

As Churchill's closed for the day, the killer hid in a locked stall in the downstairs rest-room, feet up on the toilet seat. The door to the bathroom opened as a security guard made a cursory check of the room to make sure that it was empty for the night. The killer didn't even breathe.

Hearing the door click shut, five silent minutes went by. Leaving the stall, a quick look in the mirror over the bathroom sink. So that's what a murderer looks like just before the deed is done. Wide-eyed but calm.

Stealthily, up the back stairs to the locker room, opening the door slowly and without a sound. If anyone other than Tony was there, the excuse would be simple: just lost in the maze of Churchill's building.

But no one else was there. Just Tony.

Tony was standing, back to the locker-room door. His furry headpiece sat on the bench next to his locker and he whistled absentmindedly as he pulled off the blue cossack coat. Poor stiff. Whistling one moment, dead the next.

✎ Chapter 111

B. J., you've got to snap out of it, man. You're obsessing over this. Maybe you should get some professional help.

Sitting alone in a darkened editing booth, B. J. played the tape again. At the time he shot it, he had thought it would be fun to play back for Meryl later. But there was no later.

He had made sure to get every shot Farrell could possibly want for her piece on the Paradise auction. Every costume, poster, and set design. He had shot pictures of the audience for Farrell to use later for cutaways. He had taken long shots of the auction gallery for the tape editor to choose as possible openings shots.

But at every other opportunity, when he had felt certain he was not missing something Farrell would need, B. J. had trained his camera on his girlfriend. Meryl, his lovely Meryl.

He watched the video as the beautiful woman with the dark, straight hair stood vigilant as the auction progressed. It was Meryl's job to be watchful, to do her part to make sure that everything ran smoothly.

"Beej, don't torture yourself, honey."

Farrell stood in the doorway of the editing room.

"Come on, let me take you out for dinner. It's been a long week."

"God, Farrell, I can't believe she's gone."

"I know."

Farrell put her hand on B. J.'s shoulder and together they watched the tape.

Suddenly Farrell snapped, "Roll that tape back!"

Automatically B. J. pushed the rewind and then the play buttons, and the producer and cameraman studied the television monitor.

"Look who's following Meryl out of the auction gallery!"

Chapter 112

"Federal Bureau of Investigation."

"Jack McCord, please. It's urgent."

Farrell waited what seemed like an eternity listening to the silence, praying to hear Jack's voice.

The operator came back on the line. "Mr. McCord is not in the office. But I can reach him. May I take a message for him?"

Farrell's heart sank.

"Yes. Tell him Farrell Slater called. Tell him to get back to me right away. It's very important. He has my numbers. It probably would be best if he beeped me.

Chapter 113

Tony felt something snap around his neck. Instinctively he reached for his throat, trying to pry the band that strangled him. He was choking. He heard the sounds coming from his mouth. Convulsively gasping, gulping for air. *So, this is what dying sounds like.*

It all happened so quickly. Sensing that this action would be his last, Tony dropped his hands from around his throat, reaching down behind his back. He grabbed hold of the killer's crotch and squeezed hard with all that was left of his strength.

The attacker shrieked and Tony felt the band around his neck loosen. As Tony collapsed on the locker-room floor, the killer doubled over, yelping like a wounded animal.

Chapter 114

An hour after her call to the FBI, Farrell's beeper went off and she dialed the displayed callback number.

"McCord."

"It's me."

"What's up?"

She told him about the videotape. He was quiet for a minute but he didn't sound surprised when he responded.

"That makes sense."

"What do you mean?"

"The police were just called to Churchill's. Victor Paradise left the auction house in a body bag."

Chapter 115

Jack flashed his Federal Bureau of Investigation credentials and he and Farrell were able to go right up to to Tony's room at New York Hospital. The doorman lay in his hospital bed, pale, with his eyes closed. The man's thick neck was black, blue, and angry red. Tony opened his eyes when Jack cleared his throat. They introduced themselves.

"How are you feeling?"

"Sore, and I've got a helluva headache."

"Can you tell us what happened?" Jack asked quietly.

"The guy came at me from behind," Tony croaked. "It was terrible, but I managed to grab him in the nuts." He looked at Farrell. "Sorry, ma'am."

"Don't worry about it. I've heard worse," Farrell reassured him.

"Anyway, we both fell to the floor. I managed to reach for the gun I keep in my locker and I shot him. That's all she wrote. I wasn't going to give him a chance to come at me again. Once was enough." Tony winced as he swallowed.

"Do you have any idea why Victor Paradise would try to kill you?" Farrell asked.

"No, ma'am. I've seen the guy lots of times when he'd bring his mother into the house. He always seemed like a nice enough guy."

Tony winced, the sound of his own voice seemed to be making his pain worse. Farrell and Jack leaned a little closer so Tony didn't have to strain.

"Nice," Tony continued, "but not too smart. You know, the wheel was spinning, but the hamster was dead." Tony put his index finger up to his temple and turned it around and around in the air. "We usually ended up talking about working out."

"One more question and we'll let you get some rest, Tony. Did you notice Victor Paradise talking to Meryl Quan the day of the Paradise auction?" Jack asked.

Tony tried to recall. "Can't say as I did."

Chapter 116

Clifford Montgomery opened the door to his office to let his visitor in.

"Working weekends again, Clifford?"

"What in hell are you doing here?" he hissed angrily, shepherding the visitor inside and closing the door quickly behind them.

"Relax, Clifford. Relax. My being here is not going to be a problem for you. Not unless you fail to do as I say."

Clifford glared sullenly. "Relax, my ass. How can I relax with two people killed here in as many weeks? I'd think you'd be a little more upset than you are."

"Meryl Quan had to go—she knew too much and was ready to tell. I'd think you'd be gratified that I had her taken care of."

"And Victor Paradise?"

"Victor was a stooge. Useful for pruning and clearing away the deadwood—but actually it's cleaner this way. With him gone, there's one less person to trip us up. Victor was no brain surgeon, and sooner or later he might have given something away. He served his purpose, getting rid of Meryl, and I'm sure that the police will be satisfied that her murderer is lying on a slab down at the morgue."

Clifford was stupefied by his visitor's cold audacity.

"Now, the doorman needn't be killed, even if he did see poor Victor walking out with Meryl to the freight elevator."

"You are one cold customer," Clifford observed.

"Yes. And I want my cold, hard cash. Cut me my check now."

"It doesn't work like that."

"Come again?"

"I can't just write you a check for six million dollars. It has to be done through the accounting department. The last time I inquired, they hadn't gotten the money from the buyer yet."

"Who is the damn buyer, anyway?"

"I'm not telling you. I'm more afraid of the buyer than I am of you."

The visitor tried not to lose control. *Keep calm, don't lose your temper.*

"Clifford, you don't seem to understand.

Let me explain it to you again. If you don't give me that money, I am going to let the feds know everything. Anonymously, of course. And you and your precious Churchill's will be ruined."

"But you won't have your six million dollars, either." Clifford smiled at the thought.

The visitor decided it was time to take a conciliatory tack. "Look. Let's work together here. We've always been able to work things out in the past. We can figure this out. I don't know who bought the egg, and frankly, I don't care. As I see it, the only real problem we have here is if the real Moon Egg turns up."

"If you knew who bought your fake egg at auction, you damn well would care."

Chapter 117

Farrell spread a flowered cloth over the round table and set it for two. A fresh peach-scented candle perched in a brass candlestick, and a bunch of white tulips stood at attention in a glass vase that she placed in the middle of the table. That was about as Martha Stewart as she got. Take it or leave it.

She surveyed the apartment and realized that it looked inviting now. With Pat's help, the touches they had added created a whole new feel for the room. Salmon and seafoam-green colors lay beneath the coffee table. Her books were now off the floor and arranged with care in the bookcase. Two large brass sconces hung on the wall on either side of the bookcase, apricot candles flickering welcomingly from them. A tiny oil painting of an old man reading a newspaper, a monkey sitting on his shoulder, rested on a wire easel on a mahogany butler's table, another Consignment Depot find. Farrell hadn't spent a lot of money, but the results of the few careful purchases made a big difference.

When Jack arrived, he kissed her and smelled the Pleasures perfume she had sprayed on the front of her neck and behind her ears. As she led him into the living room, he eyed the table in the small dining room beyond, appreciating the effort.

"Drink?"

"You have any scotch?"

"Dewar's on the rocks, coming right up."

Farrell poured the tawny liquid over a glass of ice and added a lemon twist.

"Ah, this hits the spot. Thanks." Jack eased himself into the couch beneath the window. He stretched out his long legs and let out a deep sigh of relief.

"So what do you think, Jack? Did Victor set the fire at Olga's?"

"Don't know. We'll have to get a picture of him and show it to the old lady."

"When will that be done?" Farrell pressed, as she stood over him.

"Hey, you," he smiled, putting down his

drink and pulling her down into his lap. "Let's just enjoy each other's company tonight, shall we? I think we deserve a little rest and relaxation."

"Not to mention a little fun, I see." Farrell kissed him hungrily, then pulled away. "But let's not get too distracted. I have a dinner all planned and you've got to realize that, for me, this is a major undertaking. I mustn't be distracted."

Jack laughed. "Okay. I can wait for dessert until later. What are we having?"

"Lamb. Lamb and asparagus and roasted potatoes."

"Farrell, I had no idea I was in the presence of such a culinary master."

"Don't make fun of me. I'm really trying here."

"I know you are," Jack relented. He stood up and walked toward the kitchen. "How can I help?"

"I thought we'd start with some of Olga's eggplant caviar. It's in the fridge."

As Jack went to the refrigerator to take out the mason jar filled with the old woman's homemade concoction, Farrell flinched with recognition, feeling the skin tingle on the back of her neck.

Eggplant—plant the egg!

Chapter 118

Range Bullock caught the late local television news Sunday evening before turning in for the night. The lead story gripped him.

"Double murder at Churchill's," trumpeted the New York anchor, who went on to recount that a female employee, and now, a patron, had both been killed at the exclusive auction house in the past two weeks.

It was time to do the story for national broadcast. As Range switched off the light, he resolved to talk to Farrell about it first thing in the morning. He hoped he hadn't made a mistake in not encouraging her to do the Fabergé egg story sooner.

Chapter 119

She could tell she was waking him up.

"Hello," Peter croaked groggily.

"Peter, it's Farrell. I'm sorry to have wakened you. I thought ten A.M. would be a safe time. I forgot what it is to be a college student."

"No, no. That's okay, Farrell. I have to get up anyway. I have one more midterm before spring break and I need to get a little more study time in. I was up late last night cracking the books. What's up, anyway?"

"Just a quick question."

"Shoot."

"Did you get at that jar of Olga's eggplant caviar yet?"

"Are you kidding? I polished that off a long time ago."

"Nothing out of the ordinary about it?"

"No, it was as good as ever. I love that stuff. Isn't it great news about Olga? She's getting out of the hospital this week!"

"Yeah, Peter. Your mom told me. That is great news. Before you know it, she'll be making caviar for you again."

"Can't wait."

"Peter, one more thing. Do you have Professor Kavanagh's home number?"

"Nope. But I think he lives in Maplewood. Maybe the operator has it."

"Thanks, Peter. I'll see you Sunday. Your mother invited me for Easter dinner."

Chapter 120

Farrell took the elevator down to the *Evening Headlines* studio, answering Range's call summoning her to the Fishbowl. She felt nostalgic. This was her last week at KEY News.

The poignant feeling that swept over her, changed to disgust when she saw that old suck-up Dean stationed on the couch across from Range's desk. She couldn't even bring herself to acknowledge him.

Range got right to the point. "Farrell, I think, with the Churchill's murders, there is enough to make a piece now, Moon Egg or no Moon Egg. I see it as 'What's Happening at Churchill's?' You'll have to be careful, have the facts to back up whatever you allege. Do you think you can get it together by Friday? I'd like to pencil you in for the 'KEYhole on America' slot. Two and a half minutes."

Farrell listened to Range's directions. How ironic! Her last story for KEY News would be a 'KEYhole' piece, the coveted slot on the broadcast. It would air on Good Friday. The anniversary of the crucifixion. Perhaps it was a sign she would rise again, another life after KEY News.

She mentally smacked herself. *Cut it out. Don't read anything ridiculous into the timing of this.*

"I can get it together by then," she answered determinedly.

Chapter 121

Farrell remembered she probably wouldn't have to deal with directory assistance to get the number in Maplewood, New Jersey. She called Westwood instead.

"Hello?"

"Pat, it's Farrell."

"Now, I told you already, you don't have to bring anything on Sunday."

"No, it's not about Easter. I should have remembered, I need Tim Kavanagh's number at home. I've been trying to reach him at Seton Hall, but it's Holy Week, and spring break begins on Wednesday."

"What's up, Farrell?"

"Oh, it's just a hunch, Pat, and I'm going to feel pretty silly when it doesn't pan out. I promise to tell you all about it when I see you on Sunday."

After scribbling it down, Farrell dialed the number that would give her the last chance to prove her theory. She listened, frustrated, to the beep of Tim Kavanagh's answering machine. Where was the professor?

Jack had looked at her skeptically when she told him her suspicion about the eggplant caviar as a hiding place. "That's what I'd call a long shot, Farrell," he said dismissively, "especially because the play on words only works in English."

Farrell had explained that she didn't think Olga had chosen the eggplant because of its semantic properties. In any event, Farrell didn't think it was that improbable.

"Tim, this is Farrell Slater. . . ." She began to leave her message. "I know this may sound crazy, but would you please check that jar of eggplant caviar Pat gave you the day we went to Olga's apartment? Let me know if you find anything out of the ordinary inside. Call me back anytime. Thanks a lot." Farrell ended by giving him her office and home phone numbers.

It was worth a shot.

Chapter 122

He made no move to pick up the phone, even as he listened intently to Farrell Slater leave her message.

He had no intention of keeping it. He had just wanted the pleasure of admiring it for a while. Imagine him, Timothy Kavanagh, having the last Russian Imperial Easter Egg! If only for a little while, he wanted to relish having the work of art with him.

Of course, he had told no one what he had found when he'd opened the mason jar. At first he had been incredulous; after all, he had watched the sale of the egg with his own eyes. Then, as he had carefully studied the glittering beauty of the milky-white egg, the treasure became real to him. There were no accidents in life. He was *meant* to have his time with the Moon Egg.

Now, a stack of essays on Russian history to correct sitting menacingly before him, Farrell Slater's message signaled that time was up. He would not call her back right away.

It would be better for it not to look as though Farrell was forcing him to give up the egg, that her call was the reason for coming forward. It had to appear that he was voluntarily giving it up to the proper authorities as he had planned to do all along.

In his darkened den, the drapes drawn closed to guard his secret, Tim had positioned a halogen lamp to warm the Moon Egg in its own special light. He looked at it now, as he had done every night since he had made the discovery, watching the diamonds and sapphires dance and sparkle. He stared at the Moon Egg, his guest for the last eleven days. His delightful, welcome houseguest. How sorry he would be to see it go!

He picked up the telephone. If he hoped to have any real future with Pat, he had to tell her what he'd found.

Chapter 123

Tuesday of Holy Week

The two old women sat together in the lounge on Olga's floor at Pascack Valley Hospital. Olga was able to walk now, and the trip down the hall to the reception room was good exercise for her.

Nadine Paradise, dressed in a beautifully-cut lavender wool suit, talked somberly to her sister.

"Now that I've lost my son, you are all I have left, Olga. I'm so grateful to God that I've found you. And so glad that you will be coming home in a few days to live with me."

"Do you have a picture of Victor?" Olga asked from her blue Naugahyde chair. "I never had a child of my own. I would like to see my nephew."

Nadine opened her smooth leather purse and carefully took a photograph from the zippered compartment inside. She looked at it sadly as she handed it to Olga.

Olga stared silently. She could not bring herself to tell her sister that the face in the photo was familiar to her. It was the face of the man who had taken care of her when she had fainted in the pharmacy. The man who had come to her apartment the day of the fire.

✂ Chapter 124

"Spy" Wednesday

It was a small group that gathered for the graveside service of Victor Paradise.

His mother stood erect, dry-eyed. Her face did not reveal the torture she felt within. How could she have raised a child capable of murder?

Nadine felt someone gently take her arm. It was Stacey. Her eyes were red-rimmed.

You thought I didn't know, but I did, reflected Nadine. *I know you wanted to be Victor's wife.* She looked up at the taller woman and smiled weakly but gratefully. She was grateful, too, for the few others who showed up. It was very kind of them. Patricia Devereaux and Farrell Slater and a man she did not recognize. He must have been a friend of Victor's. Beautiful, blue, penetrating eyes.

Chapter 125

Farrell and Jack drove back into Manhattan together after the funeral. Farrell was anxious to get back to the office. With just two days until air, she had to work on her script for the Churchill's "KEYhole" piece. She was grateful, with Passover beginning at sundown, that Dean had already explained he would be heading home early.

As they crossed the George Washington Bridge, Farrell gazed over the Hudson River, drinking in the majesty of the New York City skyline. She felt sorry for Nadine Paradise. What a cruel fate, loving and raising a child who turned out to be a cold-blooded murderer. There was no consolation for that.

Farrell was glad, though, that Nadine could have Olga now, for however long they both had. At least in the immediate future, neither woman would be alone. Farrell made a vow to herself to make sure to keep in touch with the old ladies. Perhaps, later on, she and Pat could be there to help the remaining sister when the other one passed on.

"Penny for your thoughts," Jack fished.

"Oh, I was just thinking about Nadine and Olga. Just when they have a chance to finally know each other, Nadine has to go through the heartache of losing her only child. Life. . . ." Her voice trailed off.

As the car made the turn south onto the Henry Hudson Parkway, Farrell cracked open her window to let in the spring breeze. How cool and wonderful it felt on her face. Spring. A new beginning.

Jack took her hand and held it firmly on the seat between them. Farrell appreciated the gesture, but she could not really enjoy it. Her mind had shifted into another gear as it faced what had to be done. How was she going to construct the "KEYhole" piece without the Moon Egg as concrete evidence?

She had to call Tim Kavanagh again.

❧ **Chapter 126**

Holy Thursday
Passover
April Fool's Day

The KEY News producer's arguments made sense, thought Clifford Montgomery, as he hung up the phone. As much as he detested the idea of it, and after worrying about little else all week, he knew it was right to agree to have Farrell Slater come over to interview him about all that had been going on at Churchill's.

"Okay, come over and I'll talk with you. But no camera. I'll give you my statement."

Not talking would look like he had something to hide. He knew that members of Churchill's board of directors, along with millions of other Americans, would be watching Farrell's story. It would look bad to them if the president of the auction house had nothing to say.

So he had agreed to an interview.

"Farrell Slater from KEY News is going to be here within the hour. Her piece is almost finished and she insists it is to my advantage to comment," Clifford told the visitor who sat relaxed in the leather chair on the other side of the president's desk.

"What does it matter, now that we have the real Moon Egg?"

Chapter 127

On the way out the door, Farrell decided to give Tim Kavanagh one more call. After getting his answering machine so many times, she was surprised to hear the professor himself answer.

"Oh, hi, Farrell. I'm so sorry I haven't gotten back to you," Tim apologized, "but these

last days before spring break are so hectic.
I just haven't had a chance to call you back."

I've left you at least half a dozen mes-
sages, Farrell thought. *Wouldn't it just be*
common courtesy to take a few minutes
from your busy schedule and call me back?
She tried not to sound exasperated as she
explained why she was calling.

There was silence on the telephone line,
and for a moment Farrell thought it might
have gone dead. But then Tim spoke.

"Look, Farrell, I'm going to level with you.
I did find the Moon Egg in Olga's caviar."

Eureka! With just twenty-four hours until
her "KEYhole" piece, the Moon Egg had
turned up! The proof she needed to tell the
story of the scandal of the six-million-dollar
forgery! She and B. J. could ride out to New
Jersey right away and shoot some video of
it. She was saved!

"I'm coming right out there," she told Tim
excitedly. She would reschedule her interview with Clifford Montgomery for later in the
afternoon, after she had her proof in her hot
little hands.

"Farrell, I don't have the egg anymore."

"What?" she gasped in disbelief.

"I don't have it anymore."

"Where is it?" she demanded.

"I turned it in."

"Turned it in to *whom*?"

"Clifford Montgomery at Churchill's. Pat and I decided that it was the best thing to do."

Pat? Why hadn't Pat told her? Farrell immediately wondered. But of course Pat didn't know Farrell was working on the Moon Egg story. Farrell cursed that damned promise she'd made to Peter.

She ended her conversation with Tim and immediately called the FBI. Jack was not in the office.

Again!

"Could you please tell him Farrell called? Tell him I've found what we've been looking for, and I'm on my way over to Churchill's."

Chapter 128

Security called Montgomery's office to announce that Farrell Slater from KEY News was in the lobby.

"Send her up."

"Whatever that nosey Farrell Slater comes up with, you can handle her," the visitor assured Clifford. "You don't know anything about the murders here at Churchill's, other than what the police have told you."

"And if she brings up her suspicions about the egg again?"

"Just deny, deny, deny. She has no proof, remember?"

The visitor slipped into Clifford's dressing room and pulled the door most of the way closed.

Clifford opened his office door as Farrell entered the assistant's area outside—Meryl's old spot.

"Come in, Ms. Slater. Come in."

Chapter 129

B. J. sat in a crew car parked on Madison Avenue. There was no need for the car's "NYP" tags, the license plates of the New York press corps that offered a greater selection of places to park than was available to the average citizen. With its being both Holy Thursday *and* Passover, alternate-side-of-the-street parking regulations were definitely suspended in all five boroughs of the city.

He stared at Churchill's across the street and he felt his chest tighten. Meryl.

When Farrell had asked him to come with her, B. J. had agreed, only because it was Farrell. He really didn't want to be here, didn't want to go inside where Meryl had spent so much time—the place he had last seen her.

But Farrell needed him to be close by in case Montgomery changed his mind and would talk before the KEY News camera. If she could convince the auction-house president, Farrell would call B. J. on his car phone. He could be upstairs in minutes, ready to set up and shoot.

He wanted Farrell to get what she needed for her story, but he would not be disappointed if she did not call him from the president's office. He would just as soon never go into Churchill's again.

Chapter 130

"Mr. Montgomery, I know you are a very busy man, so I won't waste your time beating around the bush," Farrell began. "The part of the story I'm most interested in here, is the auctioning of the fake egg."

"I thought you wanted to talk about the deaths of Meryl Quan and Victor Paradise."

"Well, we can talk about them first, if you like. What do you know about them?"

"Only what the police tell me."

"Okay, now we've covered that," said Farrell, eager to move on. "I know what the police tell me about the murders, too. But the police don't tell me what I need to know about this remarkable case of Fabergé forgery. The KEY News audience would only have a passing interest in the murders of two people they really don't know. They'd be fascinated, however, by the sale of a six-million-dollar forgery, perpetrated at one of the most famous auction houses in the world. What, Mr. Montgomery, do you know about the Moon Egg?"

"Ms. Slater, we've been through all this before," Montgomery sighed, with exasperation.

"Yes, but that was before I knew that the real Fabergé Moon Egg had been handed over to you."

Clifford stared at his accuser as the door of the dressing room opened silently behind Farrell.

Chapter 131

Should I go up? B. J. wondered. He sat with the car running, debating whether he should wait for her call.

She'd been inside for almost twenty minutes now. Knowing Farrell, that would certainly be enough time for her to wear Montgomery down, get him to agree to be interviewed on camera. If B. J. went up now, maybe he could help clinch the deal. *Please, Mr. Montgomery. You really should take this opportunity to speak for Churchill's, Mr. Montgomery. We can do this very quickly, sir.*

But he didn't want to go inside.

B. J. checked his watch. He'd give Farrell a few more minutes.

Chapter 132

Farrell felt something cold and hard press against the back of her head. She could feel her pulse pounding in her neck.

Clifford looked, horrified, at the two women before him. "Are you insane, Stacey?" he hissed through his clenched teeth.

"I haven't come this far to have anyone ruin it for me," Stacey snarled.

Clifford rose from his chair behind his desk and walked toward them. "It's too late, Stacey. KEY News is ready to go with the story."

"They only have the murders. Only Miss Big-Shot Producer here is trying to connect it to the Moon Egg forgery."

"You can't get away with another murder," Clifford declared desperately.

Stacey smiled maliciously. "What do you mean, 'another murder'? I haven't murdered *anybody*.

So far. Victor Paradise killed Meryl Quan.

And the jeweler, too. It was Victor who tried to kill the old lady, setting her pathetic little apartment on fire. If only he had done a cleaner job. Now, when his mother dies, she'll leave her estate to Olga. And any chance I had of coming into Nadine's fortune, such as it was, is over. Thank God I had my alternate plan. My exquisite, brilliant plan. Who would have had the courage to pull off a hoax of this magnitude? I must say I'm proud of myself."

"Stop it, Stacey, stop it. Don't say another word," Clifford demanded. "It's over."

"Don't tell me what to do, Clifford. I'm not your eager student anymore. *I'm* calling the shots now."

Stacey poked the gun harder into Farrell's skull. "You, miss, are not going to ruin it for me."

Chapter 133

B. J. watched a blue Crown Victoria pull up. Fed car. Law enforcement types like those big boats. Guess they think that size is intimidating.

Jack McCord got out of the dark blue boat.

"Hey, Jack!" B. J. called from his opened window.

The FBI agent strode over to the car, his raincoat blowing open behind him.

"Where's Farrell?" he demanded.

"Upstairs with Clifford Montgomery." B. J. motioned upward with his thumb.

"How long have they been up there?"

"Just short of half an hour," B. J. answered, checking his watch.

"Come on!" Jack shouted, as he sprinted to Churchill's heavy front doors.

B. J. grabbed his camera and followed.

Chapter 134

Farrell tried to keep herself from shaking in terror. *Keep calm,* she told herself. *Keep calm. Look for your opportunity.*

"Stacey, now I can make it right," Clifford pleaded soothingly. "I can make a swap. The real egg for the fake egg. Nobody will be the wiser."

"And just how do you think you will be able to do that?" Stacey demanded angrily.

"Stacey, you forget. The egg hasn't been paid for yet. If you don't pay, you don't get. The buyer doesn't have the egg yet. It's still here. Look, I'll show you."

Clifford went over to the wall and slid back an oil painting, exposing a safe. Quickly he spun the combination and the metal door opened, revealing the two breathtakingly beautiful Moon Eggs. They were identical.

Farrell sensed that Stacy Spinner was momentarily distracted as she viewed the

treasures side-by-side. Now was the time!
Now!

Farrell twisted around and grabbed the
gun Stacey had at her head. She caught
hold of Stacey's wrist, preventing the desperate woman from aiming. Using her head
as a ramming post, Farrell butted into Stacey's chest, pushing her backward. Stacey
fell back against the wall, but managed to
get off a shot.

Chapter 135

Jack and B. J. heard a booming shot as they
rounded the corner of the hallway outside
Clifford Montgomery's office. Jack pulled his
gun and motioned for B. J. to stay back. He
positioned himself in front of the president's
door, raised his right leg, and kicked with all
his might. The wooden panel exploded away
from the jamb, and Jack entered as another
shot rang out.

"Jack! Watch out!" screamed Farrell.

Chapter 136

B. J. shot all he could of it. Jack tackling the off-guard Stacey, wrestling her to the floor and expertly handcuffing her hands behind her back. Farrell writhing in pain, gripping her left shoulder. Blood covering the floor. Clifford Montgomery lying motionless in front of his desk. The Moon Eggs sitting side by side majestically on their blue-stone thrones in the opened wall safe.

Farrell suspected how close Stacey's bullet had come to her heart, and she was grateful. *Thank you, dear God, thank you,* she prayed. Her gratitude, though, could not eclipse the sheer joy of knowing that she had the pictures necessary to tell the most exciting story of her career.

Chapter 137

Russian Peasant Folk Belief

*"Whoever fasts on this Friday
will be saved from robbers."*

Farrell mustered all her mental and diminished physical strength as she one-handedly tapped her script into her computer. Her stomach growled, but there was no time to eat. Frustrated at the interruption, she answered her ringing telephone.

"Farrell Slater."

"It's me."

"Hi, Robbie, what's up?"

"What's up with *you*? I haven't heard from you in days."

"I'm on a deadline, Rob. I'll tell you all

about it later. But I'm glad you called. Can you pull some old black-and-white footage of the Romanovs for me? I need it for this piece."

"Okay. Sure. What's the piece about?"

Unwilling to take the time to tell him, but not wanting to brush her brother off, Farrell decided to read Robbie the script she was working on.

"What do you think?" she asked, when she had finished.

"Big sister, do I have something for you!"

❧ Chapter 138

Farrell sat in the Fishbowl Friday evening to watch *Evening Headlines*, as Range's invited guest. Her shoulder, draped with a white sling, throbbed intensely. Her brown eyes were bloodshot and tired. But she sat regally, her head held high.

For two and a half intense minutes, Farrell's eyes, and those of the KEY News staff—and, she would later discover, the

eyes of nine million American viewers—
were trained on their television sets.

For the dozenth time, Farrell watched the
piece that she had put together over the last
twenty-four hours. Eliza Blake narrated in
her trained, well-modulated voice.

"KEY News has learned that the Fabergé
Imperial Easter Egg auctioned last month at
Churchill's auction house for six million dol-
lars was a fake."

Up popped a sound bite from a spokesman from the Metropolitan Museum of Art.
"Art forgery is much more common than
people realize," he said.

Eliza appeared on camera again in a
bridge, shot earlier in the day in front of
Churchill's. "It's a story that's rocking the art
world, a story that began in the St. Petersburg of czarist Russia, wended its way
across the world, and came to an end at
Churchill's, New York's famous auction
house. A story that mixes the human emotions of greed and fear, and the all-too-
human deeds of deception and murder.

"KEY News producer Farrell Slater began
following this story last month when Churchill's auctioned an enamaled egg purported

to be the last Imperial Easter Egg commissioned to famed jeweler Carl Fabergé by Czar Nicholas II, shortly before the emperor was overthrown during the Russian Revolution. Known as the Moon Egg, it was never delivered to the czar and his wife Alexandra who, along with their five children, were executed by the revolutionaries."

Farrell had chosen some archival, black-and-white footage of the Romanovs that Robbie had pulled for her and interspersed it with material that B. J. had shot at the Russian exhibit. The large oil paintings of the emperor and empress worked well here.

"In the chaos of the Revolution, much of the contents of the St. Petersburg House of Fabergé was seized by the new government, who sold the jeweled treasures simply for the value of their precious metals and stones, unaware of—or caring little for—their artistic value. Some pieces were smuggled out of the country. Many treasures were lost completely. Some have turned up from time to time over the years."

More video of the Fabergé pieces at the Metropolitan Museum were just right there.

"That was allegedly the case of the egg that Churchill's auctioned. It was said to have been discovered at a New York City flea market. Churchill's vouched for the authenticity of the egg."

Video of the auction appeared, leading to a sound bite from Clifford Montgomery's opening remarks that day.

" 'We've had many beautiful Fabergé items that have been our privilege to auction over the years,' " said Churchill's president, " 'but none of them has matched the magnificence of the Imperial Moon Egg.' "

Eliza continued narrating the story. "On Wall Street, Churchill's stock rose on the ensuing publicity and record purchase by an anonymous buyer. But KEY News has learned that the egg Churchill's auctioned was a forgery and that the real Fabergé Moon Egg had been in the possession of the daughter of a Fabergé workmaster, the man who actually made the egg in the Fabergé studio in 1917."

Everyone in the Fishbowl listened intently as the video B. J. had shot that day which seemed so long ago at Olga's apartment, appeared onscreen.

Thank God Robbie had found it. Farrell silently resolved to give Jack the videotape box and ask him to have it dusted for fingerprints. *Dean, you're not off the hook yet, my man.*

Faithful to her promise, Farrell just used the video of the old woman's hands holding the Moon Egg; she did not show Olga's face.

"And, in another bizarre and deadly twist, police are investigating the murders of Churchill's employee Meryl Quan, and Misha Grinkov, a Russian emigré and jeweler in the Brighton Beach section of New York. Investigators now believe Grinkov made the fake Moon Egg and that both murders were committed by Victor Paradise, son of ballet legend Nadine Paradise.

"But Victor Paradise is not available for questioning. He was killed by a Churchill's doorman as he defended himself against Paradise's attack. In police custody is Stacey Spinner, an interior decorator from Saddle River, New Jersey. Authorities close to the investigation say that Spinner is the mastermind behind the forgery and the murders, and that Churchill's president Clifford Montgomery knowingly authenticated the Moon Egg forgery. Montgomery, too, is in police custody at New York Hospital where he is recuperating from a gunshot wound.

"Churchill's held an emergency meeting of its board of directors today, as the price of Churchill's stock plummeted on the New York Stock Exchange.

"Eliza Blake, KEY News, New York."

As the closing credits ran at the end of the broadcast, Range rose from his seat.

"Good work, Farrell. That's an award-winner, for sure. Thank you."

Chapter 139

Easter Sunday

Farrell popped another miniature milk-chocolate Easter bunny into her mouth.

"Keep it up," Jack warned, "and you'll have no room for Pat's dinner."

Farrell stuck out her tongue playfully. "Don't bug me. I've barely eaten in two days, and I'm starved."

"Here. If you want to try something heavenly, have one of these," Tim Kavanagh offered. "I picked up this Belgian chocolate at a little shop near the UN when I was in the city with my class last week."

Farrell chose a rich candy from its golden box and bit into it appreciatively.

"Dinner is served," called Pat, carrying a large, honey-roasted ham to the dining-room table. Emily followed along behind her mistress, eager for any table scraps that might come her way.

Farrell took a seat at the end, so that her sore arm could face out, safe from possible pokes from a dinner companion. Jack sat next to her. Across from them, Tim Kavanagh and Choo-Choo Charlie eyed each other competitively. Farrell got the feeling that Pat was enjoying having both men there, vying for her attention. Peter took his place at the head of the table and Pat seated herself at the other end, nearest to the kitchen door.

"This looks wonderful, Pat," Farrell said, observing the feast spread out before them.

At his mother's urging, Peter said grace. Finishing the prayer, he remembered to be thankful for his surrogate grandmother's recovery.

"Eat up, everybody. But save a little room. There's a big strawberry shortcake for dessert. I thought we could all take a ride up to Nadine's after dinner and share it with them. Olga came home from the hospital yesterday, you know."

It seemed to Farrell that everyone was making a concerted effort to keep the dinner conversation light. When they finished eating, they wandered into the living room and Peter switched on the television as the fanfare of the Sunday edition of *KEY Evening Headlines* began to play.

"Can't get away from the place," Farrell remarked, as she settled in to listen to the weekend anchor.

"The Kremlin announced today that the last Imperial Easter Egg, created for the doomed Russian czar Nicholas II, will be returning to St. Petersburg, the city in which it was created over eighty years ago. Russia anonymously purchased the Moon Egg for six million dollars at auction last month, withholding announcement of the acquisition until Easter, traditionally the country's most important day."

"So *that's* who bought it!" Farrell exclaimed. "But what about Olga? The Moon Egg is hers!"

Peter smiled. "When Mom and I drove

Olga home to Mrs. Paradise's house yesterday, Olga told me that a nice FBI agent had come to see her. She told him that she didn't want to make any claim on the egg. She said it's the right thing for the Moon Egg to go back to Russia."

Farrell turned to Jack. "Did you know all this?"

Jack nodded, smiling.

"And the six million dollars? Who gets that?" asked Farrell.

"No one," Jack said. "Russia isn't going to have to pay for the egg at all, which is a good thing, considering the financial mess they're in. Olga said she doesn't want the money. And Churchill's board of directors is waiving any commission that may have been earned. Smart move if they want their auction house to have any kind of future."

"Come on," called Pat, pulling on her blazer and carrying a covered cake plate. "Let's go over to Nadine and Olga's."

As the group rose to leave, Farrell took Jack's hand and pulled him aside.

"I have a surprise of my own," she whispered.

Jack waited expectantly.

"Range told me he made a mistake. A mistake he says he wants to correct. He asked me if I want my job back." Farrell tried, unsuccessfully, to wipe the smug smile off her face. It had been so satisfying to watch and listen as the executive producer admitted he was wrong.

Jack's blue eyes crinkled at their corners as he grinned down at her.

"Don't keep me in suspense Farrell," he urged. "What did you tell him?"

She shrugged, feigning indifference she did not feel. For all the arguments she'd made to herself to the contrary, Farrell knew she was not ready to leave KEY News and the world of broadcast journalism. She was relieved, grateful and thrilled to have her job back. At the same time, she wasn't about to let Range think his was her only option. Let him worry for a while.

"Come on, hot shot," Jack insisted. What did you say?"

"I told him I'd think about it and let him know."